DOUBLING DOWN

A REBEL LUST TABOO NOVELLA

OPHELIA BELL

ANIMUS PRESS

All rights reserved. No part of this book may be reproduced in any form or by any electronic means, including information storage and retrieval systems, without permission in writing from the author, except by a reviewer who may quote brief passages in review.

This is a work of fiction. Names, places, characters, and events are fictitious in every regard. Any similarities to actual events and persons, living or dead, is purely coincidental. Any trademarks, service marks, product names, or named features are assumed to be the property of their respective owners, and are used only for reference. There is no implied endorsement if any of these terms are used.

Doubling Down

Copyright © 2021 by Ophelia Bell

Cover Art Designed by Opulent Swag and Designs

Photograph Copyrights © DepositPhotos

Published by Ophelia Bell
UNITED STATES

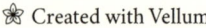 Created with Vellum

PART I
ANTE UP

CHAPTER ONE

What I had with the twins was never innocent, even though by society's standards, none of us were adults when we first started breaking the rules. We knew what we did was wrong, which only made it even more enticing. But we weren't thinking, and not thinking leads to mistakes.

Despite knowing our actions were taboo, and despite having wallowed in heartache ever since, I don't think I will ever regret the things I learned about myself that summer.

I blame myself. Maybe they blame me too; I don't know, because I never got a chance to talk to them after the fact. My parents were only fostering them, two teen boys among a houseful of kids of varying ages and backgrounds—almost all disadvantaged in some fashion.

But I was the only biological child in the mix, so it wasn't as if my parents would kick their own daughter out when they caught us.

The twins were seventeen and on the verge of aging out of the system. I was only slightly older. Legally I was an adult, and testing boundaries—my own, mostly. I could claim it was because my best friend Casey was a bad influence, but the truth was that learning a little bit about *her* dark secrets allowed me to open up the box of my own taboo desires and explore them.

That was the summer of discovery and self-condemnation, and I'm still not quite sure how to process everything that happened. Jude and Simon ran away before they got kicked out. My parents forbade me from taking the summer trip Casey and I had planned as newly minted adults. And I was stuck at home, encouraged to reflect on my mistakes while I waited for my first year of college to begin.

But Casey had already pulled away by then, which was one of the catalysts for what happened with the twins. By the time I called to cancel our trip, she had more interesting things going on anyway, so she was too distracted for me to bother filling her in on why I couldn't go.

After that, I did the only thing I could to move on: I boxed all those feelings back up and shoved them into a dark place, unsure whether I'd ever look at them again.

Three Years Later

The neighborhood where my parents live is one of those places that never changes, so when I drive home for the first summer in three years, I feel like I'm traveling back in time. The trees lining the street might be a little taller, but the houses look the same as I remember them.

A slight pang hits me when I pass the cul-de-sac where I used to spend so many days after school at my best friend's house. Impulsively I turn down the street, though I don't know why. Casey hasn't lived there since that summer three years ago when we lost touch. I heard her mom sold it and moved to another city not long after she divorced Casey's stepdad.

He isn't her stepfather anymore. That was a change I had a hard time wrapping my head around. One of my many regrets from that summer is not really listening to Casey when she admitted she was in love—really *in love* for the first time—with her stepfather Max. I probably could've gotten over her having those feelings, but then she dropped all those other bombs, and I doubt I reacted in the way she'd hoped.

I definitely didn't react the way a friend should have when she added that she was *also* in love with Max's best friend Rick, the pair of them were closet Doms, and she'd discovered she was a submissive—and was now *their* submissive.

Honestly, the first two things weren't *that* hard to process. Max and Rick were *the* hottest men in the neighborhood, and I admit to doing my share of drooling over them at summer barbecues. What girl hasn't fantasized about having two delicious, muscular, tattooed hunks like them catering to her pleasure?

It was the *submissive* part I couldn't understand. We always fancied ourselves feminists, making plans for school and careers with the hopes of being strong, self-actualized women. We didn't *need* boys. So how could Casey—a smart, beautiful, strong young woman—debase herself for the pleasure of not just one, but *two* men?

I answered that question for myself about a month after we last spoke, but by then it was too late for me to apologize. She wouldn't take my calls, and so I left for college, never putting things right between us. We haven't spoken since.

Now I can't help myself. It feels like ancient history when

we sat outside in my car after a night out, making plans for our big adventure that summer. Little did we know that her accidentally missing curfew by a mere five minutes would change everything.

As I pull closer, the house looks the same, except a new family lives there. I circle the cul-de-sac and drive out as I head to my parents' house the next block over.

Jack and Sheena Nolan—aka Mom and Dad—are borderline saints. Which is why I *still* feel a tangle of shame and guilt in my belly when I pull into the driveway, even though it's been three years since that fateful summer. I should feel guiltier about not coming home since then, but it was easy to make excuses. I had a good summer job interning at an NGO that extended through the next year as a paid spot, also earning me college credit. And besides, they could use my room to foster another child in need.

The shame I feel has nothing to do with my absence, though. And when Mom and Dad both greet me with enormous hugs, and the dogs bound across the lawn with tails wagging, and my two younger foster sisters creep out with hesitant smiles, I'm *still* anxious about stepping foot back in the house.

There are memories there. Ghosts. Bittersweet remnants of a month of discovery that turned into blame and ultimatums.

Steeling myself, I accept their love. After all, I seem to be the only one who still believes I don't deserve it.

"Baby, your room is unoccupied, so we have it all set up for you," Mom says.

"What happened to ... what was his name? Brian?" I ask.

"Bryce," Dad says. "He got adopted by a family across town about a month ago."

"So it'll just be the five of us," Mom says.

"And I'm yet again outnumbered by girls," Dad jokes.

I'm about to step through the front door when both Abigail and Hazel work up the courage to tackle me with desperate hugs.

"We missed you, Sarah!" Abby cries. "You were gone *forever*."

"I know. And I'm sorry," I say, crouching before I realize I don't need to crouch as far as before to meet the girls' eyes. "My god, you two got big."

A lump forms in my throat as I take them in. They're eight and nine now, about the age I was when Casey moved to the neighborhood and I found my first true friend.

We all head in together and I bring my things up to my old room. My stomach does a flip when I pass the door opposite mine, but when I peek in, it's no longer decked out in bunkbeds with the detritus of two athletic teenage boys strewn around. Abby brushes past into the room, bouncing on her toes, excited about showing me her new digs.

I hang with my sisters for a few minutes, trying to banish the memories. Then I head down for dinner.

Halfway through the meal, Mom offhandedly says, "Oh, Sarah, Casey called a few weeks ago asking for your number. Did she ever get in touch with you?"

My heart leaps. Casey was looking for me? I shake my head. "No. Why would she need my number? It'd be easier to just message me on social media."

"Not sure. She didn't say why she was calling. I guess she's close to graduating from Columbia. I still don't understand why you didn't choose the same school. You two were so close."

I give a noncommittal shrug. "Friends grow apart. It happens." And I really needed to just get away from New

York, so I chose a college in California instead—about as far from New York as I could get.

But when I get to my room and pull out my laptop, I give into the urge to look Casey up. Impulsively, I send her a friend request.

Then, with my heart in my throat, I type in two other names.

CHAPTER TWO

The ghosts sneak into my dreams that night in the form of hands and mouths on bare flesh. Inexperienced fingers fumble inside pajamas, skin sliding against skin.

The illicit touch of two boys I was *supposed* to think of as brothers was my first foray into the world of sex. I'd learned to masturbate a few years earlier, but it wasn't until those nights with Jude and Simon that I learned what true pleasure meant. How sweet it could be to share it with someone else, to know my touch drove them as wild as theirs drove me.

It started out as them comforting me over losing my best friend, but it evolved into so much more, until it was too big to contain. It wasn't always sex, of course; some nights we just talked, sharing our hopes for the future, making plans for after they graduated the following year. They promised to take me on that trip Casey had flaked on. They were into art, so we planned to tour all the biggest museums on the east coast, starting with MoMA, where they could see Vincent van Gogh's *The Starry Night*, Simon's favorite painting. Jude was more interested in the George Bellows collection at the National Gallery in DC.

I'd heard of *Starry Night*, of course—who hasn't?—but I had to look up George Bellows to see the hauntingly potent and violent imagery of his paintings of boxers in the ring. It made sense, since both twins were on the wrestling team and spent afternoons sparring at a local gym when they didn't have football practice.

I was looking forward to that trip so much, I started considering taking a gap year just to stay and spend time with them until they graduated. But we were reckless, and everything ended before we really had a chance to see where it would go.

We kept our trysts secret from my parents until they took a camping trip with the younger kids. The twins had summer school, so Mom and Dad left us behind, putting me in charge with the missive to not throw any parties. I obeyed that rule easily, but only because the twins and I chose to spend that week exploring our darker fantasies instead of socializing.

Suffice to say, we were so wrapped up in each other, we lost track of time and let down our guard, not realizing Sunday morning had arrived—and with it, my family.

In our defense, they *were* early. Hazel got stung by a bee and turned out to be allergic, so they'd spent the previous night in urgent care before heading home at the crack of dawn.

We were in the twins' room, having laid both their bunkbed mattresses on the floor to give us more room to play. So when Dad came in, he discovered us still asleep, tangled in the sheets with me sandwiched between Jude and Simon.

It had to have been a comical sight, in retrospect. We'd

been doing a little football player/cheerleader roleplaying after I found a couple of my old cheer uniforms. But the twins were in the miniskirts with their long hair in pigtails, and I was in the pads and helmet. We'd drifted off still half-dressed, my old uniforms stretched to oblivion from having two athletic young men stuffed into them. The football gear I wore smelled like Jude, and I claimed to never want to take it off. Gross, I know, but I was far less concerned about hygiene than about immersing myself in everything *them* that summer.

The rest of that day was a blur of anger and shame, my parents lamenting over what they did wrong, my little sisters hiding in their room. Sometime that night, Jude and Simon packed up and ran away.

They left a note, at least, but I kept it to myself out of spite, choosing to let my parents steep in worry over not being openminded enough to encourage them to stay, at least until they turned eighteen.

I didn't search for them. I think it was partly out of shame, but also due to being under house arrest without phone or internet privileges for the remainder of the summer.

I hoped they'd return, climb through my window, and steal me away—a truly absurd wish, since my room was on the third floor of our old Victorian and there were no trees or trellises for climbing. Trust me, I did a detailed survey of the house for ways to escape, but there were none.

I spent the last two weeks of summer vacation letting Mom take me to the library to check out as many romance novels as I could carry. At least *someone* was getting a happily ever after, even if it couldn't be me.

When I left for college, the seismic shift in my world was

so drastic, I managed to avoid thinking about that glorious week with the twins. But the deep-seated shame clung to me, so I used the three time zones between us as an excuse to avoid my family entirely. I made friends, and even embarked on some tepid romances that never lasted, but mostly I immersed myself in school.

It wasn't until my parents announced they were formally adopting Abby and Hazel that I finally caved and agreed to return home for the summer to help celebrate.

I adore my younger sisters, and half my guilt comes from believing I might've become a bad influence on *them*.

The sense of walking through a dream doesn't dissipate when I wake to the familiar sounds of *home*, something I haven't heard in a few years. I get a queer feeling in my belly when I lie there before opening my eyes, just listening to the rhythm of the morning.

It always begins the same way. The second the clock hits six a.m., the coffee maker's timer kicks on, it grinds fresh beans, and starts to brew. A moment later, Dad shuffles down the stairs in his slippers, unlocks the front door, and steps out to pick up the paper. Then the girls start to stir, followed by Mom.

It's comforting in its familiarity, yet I still feel like something important is missing.

I sit up and turn on my bedside lamp, then reach for my laptop where I left it at the foot of the bed. As I log into my social media account, my heart leaps at a new message from Casey.

CASEY: *!!!! Are you in town???!?*
Sarah: *Yep. Just for the summer. Back at home.*

Casey: I missed you. Like SO much. WTF happened? You dropped off the face of the planet.

I ROLL my eyes at this. She's one to talk.

SARAH: You disappeared first. Then I was grounded. Then just not in the right frame of mind for high school shit.

Casey: I hear you, neither was I. But that doesn't excuse it... for either of us. I take at least 50% of the responsibility, but I'm willing to put it behind me if you are. So... what's your schedule like? Want to meet up? I have so much to talk to you about.

Sarah: Just my sisters' adoption party tomorrow. You should come.

Casey: It's a date! But only if you promise to come out with me after. There's this place I want to show you. You might hate it, but you might LOVE it (hoping you love it, because I do). Did I mention I missed you?

I LAUGH AT HER ENTHUSIASM, and for the first time, things start to feel *normal* again. I tell her what time to show up for the party tomorrow and close the chat window, but not before checking the last one I sent last night.

My message to Jude sits unanswered, and evidently unseen. I'm disappointed, but not really surprised. I only found one twin's profile, and it didn't look like it'd been active in more than a year. If the twins are anywhere on social media, it isn't on any of the big platforms, and I'm not sure where else to look.

But *should* I even be looking? What we did was wrong. I

destroyed my parents' trust, set a terrible example for my sisters, and worst of all, I didn't fight hard enough to make my parents take care of the boys. It doesn't matter how much I tell myself they were practically adults, old enough to fend for themselves —they still needed a family as much as Abby and Hazel did.

They could've been part of *our* family, if not for what we did.

CHAPTER THREE

"I can't believe you're still driving this thing," Casey says, patting the hood of my old Honda after we extract ourselves from the party. It's mostly parents and a bunch of third-graders, so they won't miss us.

"It's served me well—two cross-country trips, and I'm hoping it'll survive a third in a few weeks."

"Holy shit, that's right! You drove it across the fucking *country*." She lets out a sigh and shakes her head. "I am so sorry I flaked on our trip. It would've been epic. I can only imagine the kind of adventure you had."

I can't help but laugh as I unlock the doors and we climb in. "It was an experience, but mostly pretty boring. It would've been more fun with a partner, for sure." I glance at her when I put the car in gear.

She gives me a sly smile and nods. "Most things *are* more fun with a partner. Or two."

"I take it that means Max and Rick are still in the picture? And that you're happy?"

Her grin widens. "Let's just say we've tested each other's

boundaries thoroughly over the past few years, and it's only brought us closer."

I pull out onto the main road and Casey directs me toward the highway. I'm curious about her unconventional relationship, but I'm not sure if I still have the right to ask about it. I'd love to compare notes, but I didn't exactly pursue something long-term with the twins.

"Where are we going, anyway?" I ask.

"You'll see," she says with a devious smile.

I can only assume it's some kind of nightclub, considering she insisted that I put on a skimpy black velvet mini-dress that drapes low in front and shows off the fanciest bra I own, something I splurged on during a weekend trip to Los Angeles with my roommate. Black satin straps that look like fat ribbons crisscross over my chest. It looks like it could be part of the dress, but it isn't. It makes me feel sexy and uninhibited, and I get a thrill from simply being seen wearing it, even though I made a vow not to get involved with anyone until I graduate from college. I don't want to risk the emotional devastation of losing someone again when I need to focus on school.

"Do Max and Rick know you're taking me out? They're cool with it?"

"Don't worry, they know. They'll be there, actually. So whatever happens, if you decide you just need to go, I'll understand. You don't need to worry about me, okay?"

I shoot her a worried look. "Okay... now I'm *really* curious about where we're going."

We're on the highway, and she directs me to take an exit that leads to a wealthy area north of the city, where all the houses have gated grounds and circular drives with acres of land between them. This is decidedly *not* the way to any nightclubs I've ever heard of.

But she keeps mum about where we're going. Frustrated, I say, "Fine, if you won't tell me, at least give me some dirt on yourself. I need to know what it's been like for you the past three years."

She waves a hand. "Oh, you know—school and work. I'm getting decent grades at Columbia. Majoring in psychology. And I get paid to have sex while people watch."

She's so blasé about her answer it takes a second for the last part to sink in. I nearly slam on the brakes.

"What? Did I hear you right?"

Casey laughs. "You did. But shit, to explain, I kind of have to tell you the truth about where we're going. Doesn't matter, though, because we're here. Turn into this driveway."

I obey, hitting my turn signal and pulling into a driveway with a fancy gatehouse blocking a drive that curves through the trees, lit with ornate lampposts all the way. I roll down my window and a man peeks in. "May I help you, miss?"

"George, it's me," Casey says, leaning over the console and waving. "This is my best friend, Sarah. I already put her on the list for a tour of Whitewood tonight."

"Ah, yes, Miss Strauss. You ladies enjoy your evening."

He presses a button to raise the gate, and I drive through, glancing at Casey. "So you're going to explain everything, right?"

"You know, it might be easier if I just show you, but I promise, *all* will be revealed." She grins as if she just made a joke, but I'm not sure I get it.

I return my eyes to the road, which is a narrow lane that winds around through dense woods. The trees finally open onto the grounds of a gorgeous Tudor mansion, well-lit from the outside. I stop at a valet stand, and someone immediately opens my door for me and offers me a white-gloved hand. I take it, too surprised not to, and step out of the car, carefully smoothing my hands down my slinky dress, then reaching back in for my purse.

"Where did you bring me, Case?" I ask under my breath as I follow her up the flagstone walkway to the house.

A muscular man in a *very* fitted suit nods at her, then leans over to open one of a pair of double doors. On my way past, I surreptitiously check him out, and wow, is he built. He also has an earbud in one ear. A second guy, similarly huge— also with an earbud—waits at another set of doors inside.

"This is where I work," she says.

I absorb the information, but it's still not quite making sense. She gets paid to let people watch her have sex. And this is where she works... in *the* most beautiful house I've ever set foot in.

We step into an opulent foyer, and I just stare at the polished mahogany paneling, silk damask wallpaper, and crystal chandelier. Two enormous bouquets of summer flowers rest on tables flanking the archway ahead of us, but on either side are two other openings, beyond which are scattered a dozen or so well-dressed people, milling around and drinking champagne while they chat.

It's the fanciest party I've ever been to, and I suddenly feel underdressed. Half the men are in suits, and all the women are in cocktail dresses that appear designer-made. I admit when I put on my Agent Provocateur bra, I felt like I might be showing off a little much, but now it seems like I couldn't have possibly gone overboard in this crowd.

A pair of men stand out, wearing worn jeans and snug cotton T-shirts. They see us standing there, and Casey waves. Some of the tension eases from my body. Thank *god*, someone I know.

Max and Rick saunter over, smiling. "It's been a while, Sarah," Max says, leaning down to kiss my cheek. He doesn't look a day older than when I last saw him, and is as hot as ever with his dark hair and devious dark eyes.

"What kept you away so long?" Rick asks, pulling me into a tight hug so I can smell the familiar scents of sawdust and varnish clinging to him—though the last time he hugged me, I was a kid.

This hug is just as innocent as they always were, though, which is comforting. Rick and Max were the DILFs of our neighborhood, but were always the nicest, coolest dudes. And I guess they never technically had kids of their own, so the term is probably misplaced. Either way, Casey could've done a *lot* worse.

"Oh, you know, school kind of monopolized my time." I wave a hand and let out a nervous laugh.

"Let's get Sarah a drink," Rick says. "She looks a little shellshocked. Case, what'd you tell her about the club so far?"

"Not much. This place is hard to describe. Easier to just give her a tour. She needs to go through the Chloe gauntlet before we can actually *show* her anything, though—you know that."

"Well, let's not waste time," Max says. He hands me a glass of champagne, then tilts his head for us to follow him down a hallway.

I take a sip of the bubbly, which fortifies me a little. It tastes expensive. "At least give me the short version so I know what to expect," I say. "I'm starting to feel a little out of my depth."

"Whitewood is a kink club," Max says. "That about sums it up."

"You mean BDSM?" I ask. After some of the secrets Casey shared with me before we quit speaking, I shouldn't be surprised, but now I'm even less sure I belong here.

"It's more complicated than that," Rick says. "It's a safe

space for a variety of kinks. Not everyone who's kinky is into bondage and discipline. For example, one of our most popular Doms is more about control. He doesn't do pain or bondage at all, but expects his subs to obey his voice alone. His subs, on the other hand, are into pain, so they often take turns playing with each other while he gives the commands. It's a trip to watch."

"We'll introduce you to all the kinks a bit later," Casey says. "For now, just be polite and honest when Chloe interviews you."

I raise my eyebrows as we stop outside a door. "Interviews me for what? I thought I was just tagging along."

"You are. But you can't go upstairs without answering some questions and signing an NDA. If you get up there and decide you want to participate, you need to be aware of the rules."

The door opens, and a distinguished-looking woman with silver hair stands there, blue eyes taking me in. "This is your friend Sarah?" she asks.

"The one and only. I trust her with my life," Casey says. "Be gentle with her, okay?"

"Wait, you're not leaving me, are you?" I ask, mild panic sinking into my gut.

Casey squeezes my arm. "I promise, as long as you're here, you never have to do anything you don't want to do. You'll be in good hands."

"Where are you going?" I ask.

"I have to go to work," she says, giving me a peck on the cheek, then turning to go with a wink. She disappears down the hallway, flanked by Max and Rick.

Blindsided by my friend abandoning me, I steel myself and look at Chloe. She gives me a warm smile.

"Don't worry, it's not as scary as you think. Come, let me give you a refill while we talk. Please, sit."

She gestures to a pair of armchairs situated near an unlit fireplace. A sheet of paper rests on the table between them, a pen laying diagonally on top of it. I sit and peek at the paper, which turns out to be the NDA Casey mentioned.

Chloe refills my drink and proceeds to grill me about my sexual history and interests. She's disturbingly thorough, but despite feeling cornered, this is the first time I feel free enough to talk about my month with the twins. I don't name them, of course; I just explain how there were two boys fostered in our house who I had my sexual awakening with. She's so accepting of the story that the level of shame I still feel seems like overkill.

"Interesting," Chloe says, a smile on her face that makes me wonder if she somehow gets off on hearing people's secrets. "And these twins… they were your age, correct?"

"A few months younger. They weren't eighteen yet. I was. Maybe that's wrong, but we were all consenting."

She waves a hand. "I believe you. I also think you will fit in quite well at Whitewood. Facilitating our patrons in exploring their secret fantasies is what we're best at."

"As fun as it sounds, I don't know if I can afford to be a member," I say, laughing. "Besides, I'm only in town for the summer. I leave for my last year of college in a couple months."

"You're a guest of one of our most popular trios. Max and Rick are two of the best Doms on my staff, and if they're willing to sponsor you, you may visit once a month at no cost. There are rules you must follow, of course. And if you want to visit more frequently, you must either pay the membership fee, or agree to perform."

Perform? Not a chance. I give a nervous laugh. "I doubt

it'll come to that. I'm just curious. It's okay if I'm just an observer, right?"

Again she smiles. "Of course. No one here is ever coerced into doing something they don't want to do. However, I will need you to sign this. It's to protect you as much as the other members and performers."

She pushes the NDA closer, then lifts the sheet, revealing a second piece of paper underneath, also with a signature line. "And please review this list. These are all the activities our members engage in while here. Please rank each one by level of interest from zero to five—five being enthusiastically interested, and zero being a hard no. At the top here is where you list your safe word."

"What do I need to do this for, if I'm not participating?" I scan the list, eyes widening at the variety of acts covered. With most there are two options, which involve both giving and receiving of every *activity*. But when I recognize several of the things I did with the twins, my panties moisten. This is a place that accepts what we did without question or judgment.

"It's to protect you, Sarah. We are very strict about maintaining the safety of our members, but on the rare occasion someone has a bad experience, we need to have a record of your hard limits. This list does *not* indicate tacit consent for any of the items on it; it's just for information purposes. I'll give you a few moments to fill it out, then I'll have a member of the staff give you the tour."

She stands and refills my glass again, then disappears through a door in one corner of her office.

"Wow, okay, I guess I'm doing this," I murmur. I glance at the champagne and push it away. I'm buzzed enough as it is. If this is happening, I want a clear head.

I sign the NDA after scanning it, then start working my

way down the list, leaving the safe word for last since that will require a little more thought. The entire time, my stomach flutters and my panties get wetter.

The first item is the benign activity of kissing and being kissed. I rank both a four, because while I love kissing, it's not what I'd call the pinnacle of pleasure for me. SM is a maybe, so three, and bondage is a four.

Genital torture is a hard zero, as is watersports or scat. Yuck.

Most of the items on the list are things I've thought about, but never done, and don't turn me off so much I'd avoid them. Few are enthusiastic fives, but the one I mark fastest is "one looking for two."

A surge of excitement rushes through me when I make the mark. It never occurred to me that I'd find myself in the position to be with two partners again, but the fact that it's a possibility—no matter how remote—makes me giddy. I doubt I'll find anything like I had with the twins, but being here isn't about finding a relationship anyway. This place is about exploring fantasies and having fun, right?

At the end of the list, I move to the top again and fill in the blank for safe word. My subconscious has been dredging up old memories of the twins this entire time, and it's as if our month of fun was only yesterday. I write "Starry Night" in the blank and nearly choke up at the thought of how much they'd have loved this place. If only we'd found it together.

Then I stand and wander to the nearby bookshelf, perusing Chloe's library. I expect books about sexuality, but mostly find classics, though some are decidedly racy classics like *Fanny Hill*, *Lady Chatterley's Lover*, or *Delta of Venus*.

The door opens and I turn, smiling at Chloe. "I finished the list."

"Wonderful. Then I will leave you in the capable hands of

my tour guides." She steps aside and motions toward the door.

As if she's read my mind, not one, but *two* men step through. They're tall, clean-cut, muscular... and they're twins.

Not only that, they're *my* twins.

CHAPTER FOUR

"Sarah?" Jude's mouth falls open and he stands there, staring at me. Simon enters behind him and rocks back as if he's been struck. I'm just as stunned.

They look *good*, though—less like the seventeen-year-old boys they were the last time I saw them and more like full-grown men. Their hair is short now, cropped almost to their skulls, and they're dressed in tailored suits and crisp white dress shirts, looking every bit like they belong in this place with all these well-dressed people.

There are more new details: I see a hint of a tattoo peeking above the collar of Jude's shirt, stark black against his deep tan, and both twins have small silver hoops in their ears. Jude has another hoop through his right eyebrow, while Simon has one in his left nostril.

"What..." I stop, not sure what the hell to say. "What are you guys doing here?" I finally manage, because seriously, why are they *here*, of all places?

They glance at each other, then at Chloe, whose smirk and raised eyebrow tells me she's put the pieces together.

"These two are the boys you mentioned, aren't they? What an amazing stroke of fate."

Jude frowns. "You told her about us?"

My face heats. "It was part of the interview. I didn't see the point in lying. But the last thing I expected was to see you again, like *ever*."

A lump forms in my throat as the heartbreak of their departure washes over me anew. They had a good reason to go, but it still hurt like hell when I never heard from them again.

"We work here," Simon says. "Have for almost three years now."

"So you know Casey?" I ask, though my mind is fixated on *what* they do here more than who they know. And more importantly, who they do it to.

My stomach lurches at the idea that all this time they might've known Casey, and she didn't mention them to me before bringing me here. Or that they might *more* than know her...

"Yeah? Everyone knows Casey," Jude says, frowning and looking at his twin.

"Oh god," I mutter, a chilly prickling sensation working its way up the back of my skull.

I can't be here now. This is too much, too fast. I turn and stride to the door, aware of nothing but the driving need to escape. But the feeling that my world has just dropped out from under me doesn't end when I make it down the hall, or out the door to the valet.

"Sarah, wait!" one of the twins calls as I slide into the driver's seat and slam my door.

I speed off, leaving them standing in the driveway in my rearview mirror, each of their faces perfectly mirroring the other's shocked expression.

I don't know what any of it means, and I struggle to make sense of it as I try to find my way back to the highway. I took Casey's news in stride. Before she dropped out of touch, she told me what had happened between her and Max, so the fact that she's now a member of some crazy, secret sex club isn't that strange a concept.

But the twins… How did this happen? My sweet, attentive boys, so curious about what would make me feel good… How did *they* get mixed up with that place? Not that any of us were exactly innocent, but I still think of them that way.

I corrupted them. If anything, it's *my* fault they wound up there. God, what did I do to turn them into… whatever it is they've become?

I'm so lost to my memories I don't realize until I pass an unfamiliar signpost that I have no clue where I am. Without Casey to help me navigate back the way we came, I must've gotten turned around somewhere outside the safety of the affluent neighborhood she directed us to.

The road has gotten dark and winding, with nothing but trees on one side and a guard rail on the other. I spy an overlook and pull into it to try to get my bearings, but instead of taking out my phone to look at the map when I stop, I just cut the engine and sit there, staring into the darkness interrupted by the twinkling lights of a small township in the valley below.

I suddenly feel like an idiot for running the way I did. I've spent the last three years trying to put the twins behind me while still harboring an unending ache for what could have been. I only decided to come home because I felt like I'd finally succeeded in forgetting that summer, in solidly locking my eyes on the future and my career after college. The NGO I intern for always hires from the pool of interns, so I'm pretty much guaranteed a spot with them once I graduate. I'm *going* back to California; there's no question.

So why did seeing the twins again shake my convictions so thoroughly? It's not like we can pick up where we left off. It's not like I'm suddenly going to change all my carefully made plans just to fuck up the way I did after high school. That can*not* happen.

I bang my head on the steering wheel, because despite all these thoughts, I can't get the image of the men I just saw out of my head. I can't get all the fucking *questions* out of my head. But it's too late now. I ran, so I have to deal with it.

I reach for my phone to figure out where the hell I am. Just as I tap the screen to pull up the map, the rumble of an engine approaches from down the road, and then a headlight fills my rear window, blinding me when I glance in the mirror.

Just one headlight—a motorcycle, judging from the sound of the engine. But a moment later, it's joined by a second, and instead of riding right by, they turn into the same overlook, pulling up on either side of my car.

My adrenaline spikes, and I hit the door locks and hunch down with my phone clutched in my hand, ready to dial 911. The rider on my side climbs off his bike and pulls off his helmet, then bends down to peer in through the window.

"Sarah? It's just us. Will you stop and talk?"

It's Jude's handsome face beyond the glass. Turning to the other side, I see Simon peeking in the passenger window, and my tension eases, but only enough to let the earlier tangle of emotions return.

"You guys scared the shit out of me!" I smack the window, pissed now as I disengage the locks, grab the door handle, and push it open so fast Jude has to step back to avoid me nailing him. "What the fuck?"

"Sorry!" He backs up to his bike, hands raised. "We just couldn't let you go without talking to us. I was afraid we'd lose our chance and go three more years without hearing from you. Do you have any idea how wrecked we were the last time you cut us off?"

My eyes widen. "Cut *you* off? You *ran away* and only left me a note! I never heard from you again. It wasn't as if you didn't know where I lived, for Christ's sakes!"

Simon rounds the front of my car and stands by his brother, eyes filled with wonder as well as pain. It's that look that makes my anger ebb.

"We couldn't show our faces there, and you know it," Simon says, his voice more subdued than his twin's. "Neither of us were willing to call and risk having to talk to Mr. Nolan or your mom. We figured it was probably better for you if we kept our distance. I guess we just hoped you'd reach out."

I swallow hard and shake my head, tears threatening. "It wasn't better for me. The rest of the summer fucking sucked, which is why I left. I was a *mess* after that. I second-guessed everything for months. I was so lost."

A tear escapes, and I swipe angrily at it. Jude steps close and raises a hand wrapped in a fingerless leather glove. He cups my cheek, brushing his thumb across the tear. His eyes search mine, and I find it hard to breathe looking back into those dark, anguished depths.

"God, Sarah. If you only knew what it was like for us. We never got over you. I still…" He stops and takes a fortifying breath. "I still think about you all the time. Seeing you is like a dream. You're even more beautiful than I remember."

His gaze drifts down from my face, lingering at the top of my bodice before dropping lower and sliding back up. His nostrils flare, and I can't help but tilt my head into his hand the slightest bit. His touch is electrifying; I've spent so long wanting exactly this, believing I'd never have it again.

"Jude..." My entire body involuntarily arches closer, and the next thing I know, he's kissing me, cupping the back of my head with one hand while he slides the other around my waist, pulling me tight against him.

He feels different, but tastes the same as I remember—like gingersnaps. His tongue teases just like I remember too, teeth nipping at my lip the tiniest amount, a trick that always sent sharp jolts straight to my core. This time is no different, and the strength of his embrace just adds to my need.

I get lost for several moments, forgetting everything. The last three years of regrets fall away entirely, and when I pull away to catch my breath, Simon fills the gap, grabbing me by the jaw with both hands and angling my head to take my mouth in a bruising, hungry kiss. I hook an arm around his neck while still holding onto Jude, leaning into Simon's warmth while he plunders my mouth.

Jude glides his lips down my jaw to my throat, the pair of them as in sync as they ever were. He nips at my collar bone, then peels off a glove and cups my breast through my dress, molding his hand around it.

"Goddamn, you feel better than I remember," Jude says. He nuzzles the top of my breasts and tugs at my bodice. It's stretchy and gives easily, my fancy bra still covering me.

"Jesus, this is sexy," he says, sliding fingers between the wide, dark strips of ribbon and my heated skin. His knuckles skim over my nipples, and he tugs the bottom of the bra down. My nipples hit warm air for a split-second before Jude wraps his lips around one, his fingers around the other. I throw my head back and moan, forcing Simon to release my mouth.

Jude pushes me backward against the fender of my car,

and I'm grateful to have something solid on which to brace myself. Simon's gaze drops to where his twin toys with my breasts. His eyes go dark and he pushes Jude's hand aside, taking over with his mouth on my other breast.

I rake my fingernails lightly along his neck and up his scalp, marveling at the difference from the last time I saw them. Their hair was always so gorgeous, shoulder-length and thick, almost black. It's as soft as I remember, but too short to grab hold of, so I just touch, too in awe of their very existence to stop.

"I can't believe you're really here," Simon says, rising to look into my eyes. "Is this even real?" He takes my face in his hands again, staring down at me.

I nod, then gasp as Jude finds his way beneath my dress with one hand, stroking his fingers lightly between my thighs before grazing a fingertip just beneath the edge of my panties. Then he lifts his hand and holds it up to his brother's nose.

"Does this smell real enough to you?"

Simon's nostrils flare as he inhales, then hums, his mouth quirking wickedly and feral desire filling his gaze. He drops to his knees then and grabs me by the leg, hooking my knee over his shoulder as he shoves my dress up. Jude chuckles and slides his finger into his mouth, sucking it clean.

"He always got drunk on your scent," Jude says. "I preferred watching you fall apart as much as being the cause of it."

Simon presses his face between my thighs, nipping my engorged flesh through my panties. He grabs hold of the waistband of the skimpy lace and tugs down just far enough to insert his tongue at the top of my crease. Hot wetness floods my core as he presses his tongue tight against my clit.

I gasp and cling to Jude, who leans in for support,

watching his brother destroy my will with his tongue before dropping his mouth to my breast again.

"Oh god," I moan. It was never this good before—never so overwhelmingly perfect. I don't even care that we're out in the open, by the side of the road, and that anyone might drive by and see us.

Simon tugs my panties down a little lower, then gets frustrated by the barrier and yanks hard with both hands. One side snaps and they fall, dangling around my upraised thigh as he descends on my pussy again, this time plunging his tongue between my folds and flicking it hard against my clit. My desire rises so fast it makes my head spin, but Jude is there, holding on tight, his mouth at my ear as my orgasm takes hold.

"That's my girl," he murmurs. "You remember how much we love it when you don't hold back. Tell me you're ready for more. Please fucking say you want more."

"I want more," I pant, legs trembling.

"Turn around, baby," Jude says, and I can't do a thing but obey.

When Simon rises, he helps me pivot, and then they both bend me over the hood of my car. My nipples hit cold steel, and one of the twins lifts my dress. With my panties gone, the warm summer breeze gusts across my wet pussy, stoking my heat high once again.

I have never been more eager, more ready to be fucked in my life.

CHAPTER FIVE

I wait an eternity, but don't hear a zipper.

"Fuck me, I don't have a condom," Jude mutters. "Do you, brother?"

"She caught me as off-guard as you," Simon says.

I peek over my shoulder to see them both staring longingly at my ass. "It's okay," I say. "I'm on birth control. And that interview I took made it sound like you guys have to prove you're clean to work there, right?"

The realization hits them both simultaneously, their gazes darkening. Jude cocks his head and reaches out, gliding his fingertips up through my sensitive channel. His fingers graze my ass the tiniest bit, which sends a fresh throb of need to my clit.

We tried *everything* when we were together, including anal, which was gross to think about until we tried it and learned how epic my orgasms could be. They loved that they could both be inside me at the same time too. I'm positive Jude's remembering how it felt, but he still doesn't make a move.

"What's wrong?" I ask. Neither twin looks like he plans to back out, so I'm not sure why they're hesitating.

"Nothing. Not one fucking thing," Jude says. "I just want to savor this moment. We always used condoms before. I want to enjoy not having to use one for the first time."

Simon claps his brother on the shoulder. "Just don't take all night. I need a taste too." He leans over the hood and curls his hand around my nape, then kisses me again. I sigh into it, near tears at how perfect it feels.

Finally I hear the clank of a belt buckle and a zipper, then Jude gently rests both hands on my ass, gliding his thumbs down the crease and gripping a little tighter as he spreads me open. One hand disappears, and he presses his his thick, hot tip to my opening.

I moan and tilt my hips to signal how ready I am, but he seems determined to draw this out. Once he notches his cockhead at my entrance, he returns his hand to my ass, gripping for leverage as he pushes in so slowly it makes my head spin.

"Jesus fucking Christ, you feel so good." He practically groans the words as he seats himself deep inside me. I clench my muscles around him, enjoying the moan he gives in response before he begins to move. Then it's my turn to moan into Simon's mouth as my need is stoked. Every slow thrust of Jude's cock drives me higher, closer to another climax.

Simon releases my mouth and brushes soft kisses over my jaw. He continues clutching the back of my neck as he presses his mouth to my ear.

"I remember how tight you were the first time we fucked you—how greedy that hot little pussy was for two big dicks. I missed you so much, Sarah. It's going to be so, so good now that you're home. You're a fucking dream come true, and I can't *wait* to get my dick into you."

"Simon," I whine, reaching for him. Some muddled part of my brain manages to react to the part where I'm home. Because I'm not… not really. I'm only here for a few weeks before I go back to California.

But I don't want to think about that right now—not when I've found them again after so long. I want to be their toy and have them be mine, the way it was *meant* to be between us. But mostly I just want to be with them, one hundred percent free from worry about what we are to each other. They might have been like brothers the first time, but they are decidedly *not* like that now.

I'm at the edge again when Jude picks up his pace, his thick shaft driving right across my G-spot with every thrust. I need to come, but can't without at least a little stimulation to my clit, which he doesn't give me. But I don't mind.

Jude lets out a deep groan, his cock flexing and shooting deep inside me. The very second he pulls out, Simon moves in, slamming home within seconds. The force of his first thrust makes me cry out, and I press my palms against the hood, pushing back. He fucks me with abandon, pulling no punches as he groans and squeezes. He's the dirty, wild twin, the one who always came up with the most depraved experiments we could try with each other. So it's no surprise when his thumb breaches my rear entrance and he starts fucking into me there too.

I'm done for when Jude strokes my hair and looks into my eyes. "You ready to come?"

I nod, too lost to pleasure to form words, but he knows what I need. He slides his hand between my thighs from underneath and finds my clit.

"Jesus, you're all engorged. I always loved how big your clit gets when you're turned on."

He strokes the swollen bundle, then pinches lightly and rubs. I gasp as the pleasure jacks through me like a fresh shot of adrenaline.

Simon groans as my pussy clenches around him involuntarily. Jude keeps toying with my clit, doing all the things he learned to do to drive me insane before. With his expert fingers stroking me and Simon's cock in my pussy, his thumb buried in my ass, I lose it completely. I scratch at the hood of my car as I fly over.

Simon's right there with me, burying his face in my neck as he spills inside me. He grips my hips hard with both hands, holding me tight against his groin as his cock continues to pulse. I lay gasping, my cheek to the hood, staring into Jude's eyes as he props himself on one elbow and gazes intently back at me. He strokes my cheek, then leans in, kissing me again, slowly this time.

"We have a lot to talk about," he says. "Will you come home with us?"

My heart pounds just a little harder. As sated as I am, the tangle in my belly leaves me at odds on how to answer. I'm desperate to know everything, but terrified of what I'll learn.

"Don't you have to work?" I ask.

Simon pats my ass as he pulls out, then tugs my dress back down to cover me. My ruined panties fall to the ground, and he bends to pick them up. I don't miss the private smile on his face when he tucks them into his pocket.

"We're due a night off," Jude says. "I think, under the circumstances, Chloe will understand. So... will you?"

Somehow I'm looking for another excuse to say no, which is ridiculous. I can't claim curfew, because I'm old enough not to have one anymore. My parents think I'm with

Casey, so it wouldn't be weird if I texted to say I'm staying over with her. As far as I know, nobody in the neighborhood is aware of her situation with Max and Rick. She claims they're super-careful about how they appear in public. She lives on campus with a female roommate, so it's easy enough to keep people in the dark. I wonder if her roommate knows…

But I don't like keeping secrets, especially from my parents, and I don't want to lie to the twins either. I clench my eyes shut. "Ugh, yes. I want to. But I'm letting my parents know where I am. I'm not leaving it to chance this time."

Simon frowns. "Sarah, do they really need to know?"

"No, but the alternative is lying to them, which I promised myself I'd never do again after last time. If they can't deal with it, it won't change anything, but they deserve to know."

I push past him and open my car door, reaching in for my phone where I left it on the driver's seat.

I send a quick text, but don't wait for a reply. When I glance up, both twins are staring at my phone.

"What'd you tell them?" Jude asks.

"That I ran into you guys and I'm going home with you to finally talk about what happened three years ago. They can infer whatever they want from it. I also said I might not be home tonight, and not to worry."

They glance at each other, and their hesitation is palpable. I can't help but laugh. "Guys, you were impulsive enough to bend me over my car just now and fuck me. Why does this scare you?"

"We haven't exactly associated with many people as straightlaced as your folks in a really long time," Simon says. "As much as I love the fact that you seem to be way more independent now than you were back then, it still terrifies me."

"Well, I've been the model of a perfect daughter for the past three years. I feel like I've earned some trust. I don't plan to destroy it again by doing shit behind their backs. If you two can't deal with it, then I guess I can just go home."

I climb into my car and start the engine.

"Wait!" Jude bends down and peers in at me. "Follow us, okay? Don't go home. I'm afraid if you do, I'll never see you again."

I melt a little at the desperate quaver in his voice. He still can't tell when I'm bluffing, but when I glance at Simon, the slight smile he gives me tells me he knows I'm full of it.

"Okay," I sigh. "Lead the way."

PART II
DOUBLE DOWN

CHAPTER SIX

I follow them back down the winding mountain road until the scenery becomes familiar again. It's *too* familiar, in fact. I'm not sure what I was expecting, but when they turn into my neighborhood, I think they must have lost their minds and decided to go home with *me* instead of the other way around.

But we don't turn down my parents' street. Instead we take another turn a block later, and it hits me where they're headed.

A few minutes later, they turn up a short gravel driveway at the far edge of the subdivision where the trees get thicker. Beyond the tree line is hilly wilderness. It's one of the most peaceful places in my old neighborhood—a place Casey and I used to explore as kids.

A pretty arts and crafts home rests in the center of the lot, surrounded by meticulous landscaping. The porch light is on, but I know no one is home. This is where Max and Rick live; it's the house Rick bought with his late wife ages ago and remodeled. She passed away about five years after they got married, so he lived alone until Max moved in after his divorce from Casey's mom.

I've been here dozens of times over the years when Rick and his wife would host neighborhood barbecues, so I get a blast of nostalgia when the twins pull past the house to the big building nestled in back. Rick's woodshop was always a wonderland of interesting stuff. He would set up projects for the younger kids during the parties, safely stowing all the more dangerous tools and just letting them go to town with paints and glue and scraps of wood.

"You guys live here?" I ask, walking around my car to face them after I park.

"Yep. We have ever since ... well, since that night, I guess," Jude says. He tilts his chin up a set of stairs attached to the outer wall of the woodshop. They lead to a small covered porch, warmly lit with a light that illuminates the trailing vines of night-blooming flowers clinging to the posts.

"Rick took a big risk on us," Simon says. "When we left your house that day, he caught us hitchhiking and brought us home with him, no questions asked. He set us up in the workshop loft, gave us a place to live, food to eat. He had us doing odd jobs to pay for our lodging. At first it was just cleaning up, doing yard work, that kind of thing. We started assisting him with some projects, then eventually he asked if we wanted to be his apprentices."

I frown. "Casey knew all this time that you guys lived here?" I'm a little pissed at this revelation. How could she not tell me?

The twins share a glance and Simon narrows his eyes. "We never talked about what happened with you. We didn't think it was right to share our secret. And when we got here, the two of you were already not speaking, so it was easier to just not talk about it. Then she moved to a dormitory on campus, and we only ever saw her at the club... which is not exactly the kind of place you have heartfelt discussions about old friends."

"But we're speaking *now*," I say, stomach sinking at the reminder of that fateful summer when everything went to shit. "She could've told me tonight."

"It's been three years, Sarah. I'm sure if she'd known what we were to each other, she would have said something," Simon says, spreading his hands to try to appease me.

My chest tightens, and I feel tears coming on. I nod because I know he's right; Casey would've said something, had she known. "Well, I'm glad Rick found you. I worried..."

The words won't come after that, and I just shake my head, wiping my eyes.

Jude closes the distance and pulls me into his arms. "We did all right, Sarah. It might've been the best thing that ever happened to us."

"Ugh, that's a relief, but I still feel like shit," I say, my voice muffled by his shoulder. His leather jacket smells like him, and the awareness hits me deep. I slide my arms underneath and wrap them tight around him, reveling in how warm and solid he feels.

He gives me a soft peck on the cheek and says, "Can we show you our place? We've gotten it pretty dialed in. And there's more I want to show you, but maybe not until tomorrow? That is, if you'll spend the night."

"More than your place?" I look up into his eyes to see a familiar mischievous glint. Now I'm intrigued.

"I take it that means you're staying," Simon says with a smirk. "But we'll save the *more* for tomorrow. C'mon."

He starts up the steps and pulls out his keys to unlock the door. The entire place smells like freshly cut wood. I never realized how comforting that fragrance was until now. But inside the loft, I'm hit with a scent that is purely *them*. It's like walking into a memory, and I close my eyes for a second just to absorb it.

They were athletic boys, so there's still that faint musk of sweat, but it's nowhere near as bad as the dorm rooms of some of my male college classmates. I smell wood, and coffee, and ginger and cinnamon.

"You okay?" Jude asks, nudging me gently.

I take one last deep breath and nod. "I missed you guys."

"We missed you too," Jude says, tugging me close and nuzzling my hair. "So much."

"Let me give you the tour," Simon says. He points to the right, where a purple velour sofa rests beneath a long row of windows. "Living room." Then to the left, to a kitchen peninsula and the small galley kitchen. Its backsplash is made up of cheery yellow tiles, and it's got a cutting board countertop, above which a window overlooks the backyard.

"Kitchen," he says. "And where we're standing is the dining room." He pats a small table that looks like it might expand to fit more than two.

Jude takes over, walking farther in. "This is our office," he says, pointing out two desks facing each other by more windows. The entire floor plan is open, aside from an accordion-style partition between the living room and office. "Bathroom's through there."

I peek through the door to see a bathroom that is spacious and mostly new, with double sinks and ornate painted tiles on the counter. A huge, claw-foot tub rests beneath the singular window. In the corner beside it is a large, glassed-in shower stall with artsy tiles that match the counter. A potted plant sits between the toilet and the tub, making it feel even more like a small spa retreat.

I step back out and follow the twins. Just before the final

door is a small corridor with a closed door at the end. "What's that?" I ask.

"Stairs down to the shop," Jude says, "so we don't have to unlock the main door to go to work."

The last door leads to the bedroom, which is the only room that still looks like a pair of teenage boys live in it.

"Oh my god. You guys still sleep in bunkbeds? That's... so precious."

Simon's cheeks flush. "Well, we don't exactly *entertain* much."

"Ever. He means to say we don't entertain *ever*. You're the first woman who's ever been up here." Jude crosses his arms and leans on the bedpost. It's a pretty *large* set of bunkbeds with full-size mattresses—and it makes sense, since there's more room to move around—but they're grown men. How have they never *dated*?

I blink, my mouth falling open. "Seriously? But... the club. And you guys know Max and Rick are like—kinky, right?"

They both laugh, and Simon gives me an indulgent nod. "Yes, Sarah, we're aware of that. We're not monks. We just don't bring it home. Our, ah... *apprenticeship* has extended beyond woodworking, but one of the rules our teachers set was to maintain a safe distance between the fun we have at the club and what we do in our private space."

"Oh." I nod, not sure how I feel about that. It confirms my impression that they *do* fool around with other patrons of Whitewood. To what extent isn't clear.

"We'll tell you anything you want to know," Simon says. "Come back out and let me get you a drink. We can sit and talk for a bit, if it helps."

"God, yes. That would be great. Can I just use your restroom first?"

"Make yourself at home," Jude says while Simon disappears back to the main room. "If you need *anything*, just ask. I mean that."

"Um..." I hesitate in the bathroom doorway, glancing down at my stilettos and slinky dress. "Would it be weird if I asked to borrow some sweats? I'd kind of rather not lounge around in this."

"I'm on it," he says, slipping into the bedroom.

I step inside and close the door, then do my business and clean up a bit from our epic fuck earlier. My entire body tingles when I wipe, because my pussy is still tender and slightly engorged. Just being near them does this to me.

Despite my lingering questions, I'm overwhelmed with a sense of rightness about being here tonight. The second I walked into their space, I felt like I was *home* in a way I didn't feel walking into my own house. It isn't the place, either—it's *them*.

I decide to let go of the worry for tonight, because I just don't want to know. If this is going to be my only chance to enjoy them, I'm going to milk it for everything it's worth.

So I make myself at home, just like Jude said. I strip out of my dress and turn on the shower. The tub is tempting, but I really just need a few minutes of heat and solitude to absorb the events of this evening and gather my thoughts.

They have the same soap they've always used, of course, and I'm pleased to see they keep a bottle of the same conditioner, even though they cut off their beautiful locks.

I'm rinsing my hair when I hear a soft knock on the door, and then Jude pokes his head in.

"Everything okay?" he asks.

"Yeah, sorry." I laugh and swipe at the steamy glass. "I couldn't resist. This bathroom is amazing."

"This was six months' worth of rent, so we made it worthwhile. I'm glad you like it."

His gaze coasts down my body and he steps into the bathroom, grinning.

"What are you doing?" I ask when he begins to unbutton his shirt and kick off his shoes.

His grin widens. "I have fantasized about having you in here ever since we finished it. Remember the first time we showered together?" He drops his pants and briefs, then steps in with me.

"We had a lot of firsts together, didn't we?" I trail off, because breathing becomes difficult the way he fills the space. Somehow he's even bigger naked.

"I think that was my favorite first." He grabs the body wash and squirts some into his hand, then starts soaping up his chest. I'm mesmerized by the sight of his big hands sliding over his muscles, and indulge in taking in every single beautiful inch of him.

"You filled out," I say, eyeing his thick pecs and broad shoulders. The tattoo that skates up his arm is a kaleidoscope of color and abstract patterns that enhance the shape of his bicep, and I impulsively reach out and graze my wet hand up to his shoulder.

"You're still the most beautiful woman I've ever set eyes on," he says, stepping closer until his erection grazes my belly.

My breath hitches as he lifts a soapy hand to cup my cheek, and I tilt my head back, accepting the wet kiss he presses to my lips. I open for him and lean back, arching into him. Water cascades over our heads, into my mouth, and I swallow it along with the moan he gives me when I reach down to wrap my hand around his shaft.

"Jesus," he murmurs, then lets out a gasp when I squeeze him. He stares at me with hungry eyes. "I bet I can hold you up on my own now."

I lift an eyebrow and smile. Last time we had sex in the shower, I was a little heavier, and he wasn't quite so built, but we had fun, nonetheless. Simon joined in, and I found myself suspended between them both while they took turns fucking me beneath the hot water.

"What about Simon?"

He tilts his head back and bellows, "Yo, Simon! I'm gonna fuck Sarah in the shower, if you want in on this!" Then he grins down at me.

"You're crazy!" I say, laughing as I embrace him.

The door opens a split-second later and Simon steps in, three glasses of wine in his hands. He sets them on the counter before hopping up to seat himself. He swings his feet and makes a little circle with his hand.

"Thanks for the invite. Don't stop on my account. I'm in the mood to watch for a bit."

"You sure, dude?" Jude asks warily.

"Yep."

Jude meets my gaze again with a lazy smile. "Don't trust him," he murmurs. "He's going to try to bogart you later."

"Would that be so bad?" I ask, glancing over Jude's shoulder at Simon, who's sipping his wine. He winks at me from his perch, and I grin, then meet Jude's gaze again.

"Maybe I worry I'm not enough for you," Jude says. "I remember how insatiable you were. You wore us out."

"You're older now, so no doubt you have more stamina. Try me."

He looms close, skating his hands down my sides. I comb my fingers through his wet hair and let out a surprised gasp when he suddenly hoists me in his arms and presses my back against the wall behind me. I hold onto his shoulders as I wrap my legs around his waist, locking my ankles behind him.

"You ready?" he asks.

I nod, and he wastes no time positioning himself and slamming in deep.

"Oh, fuck!" I cry, instantly awash in mind-numbing pleasure as Jude starts to fuck hard and fast. I can't help but laugh with pure joy at his enthusiasm, and he swallows my laughter with a kiss that makes my head spin.

"God, I missed you," he says, hiking me up a little higher so he can impale me even deeper.

My eyes meet Simon's over Jude's shoulder, and I bite my lip as he licks his own and sets down his wine, then grabs the bulge at the front of his pants and readjusts it. He doesn't touch himself more than that, but the ridge of his erection holds my attention as his twin nails me to the shower wall.

But Jude was right—he isn't enough.

"Stop," I whisper, eyes still fixed on Simon as I tap Jude's shoulder. He immediately pulls out and sets me down.

"What is it?" he asks.

I don't answer, merely push through the shower door and drop to my knees in a puddle between Simon's thighs. I grab for the button of his fly, and have his pants open and his cock out a second later.

"Fuck, Sarah," Simon mutters, tilting his hips toward me as I wrap my mouth around the head of his cock. "Fucking fuck, oh, *fuck*."

He slides halfway off the counter to give me a better angle, and I take his length deeper, one hand wrapped around his shaft while I yank at his pants with the other.

He rips off his shirt, then shoves his pants down and gently rests his palm against the back of my head, guiding me, even though I remember exactly how he likes to be sucked.

"Not cool," Jude says. The noise from the shower ceases

and he steps into my periphery, still dripping wet and hard as steel.

I pull back from Simon and divert my attention, reaching for Jude and sucking him deep.

"Ohhhkay, I guess you're forgiven," he says with a low chuckle, followed by a grunt when I deepthroat him.

I keep one hand on Simon's shaft, stroking him while I suck Jude for a minute, then switch again. They scoot together to make the switch easier, and I divide my attention evenly, marveling at how at least this part of them hasn't changed a bit. I'd become very well-acquainted with both their cocks, and how to suck them off is as easy to recall as riding a bike.

"Sarah, let us come on you," Jude says. "I want to cover those gorgeous tits with my spunk."

Holding each cock in one hand, I smile up at him. "I wouldn't have it any other way."

It takes only a few quick strokes, and first Jude's, then Simon's cock erupts across my chest, painting my skin in sticky, creamy stripes.

Naturally the mess earns me a second shower, but this time, *I* am the focus of *their* attention.

CHAPTER SEVEN

We manage to deplete the hot water in their shower, but not before they thoroughly reciprocate the attention I just gave them. They bracket me beneath the spray, one in front and one in back, and I drape one leg over Simon's shoulder, holding onto the wall for balance while they utterly destroy my pussy and ass with their tongues. My legs are jelly when I climax, to the point that Jude has to stand and support me from behind while Simon takes his sweet time soaping me up and washing every inch of my bare skin.

He ends the bathing with his fingers buried in my pussy, finger-fucking me to yet another orgasm.

"God, I missed the sounds you make when you come. I missed the way you don't hold back. That's right, dig your claws into me. Let me hear you scream."

It's as if a dam I didn't know I'd built has crumbled, setting free every pent-up desire I've had for the past three years. I cling to him, crying out as he pushes me over the edge while Jude squeezes my breasts and pinches my nipples.

We can't ignore the chilly water anymore, though, and

I'm nearly blue despite the heat of pleasure still coursing through my veins.

I let them bundle me into a giant fluffy robe and lead me into the living room, where they deposit me in the center of the giant purple sofa and hand me my wine.

I'm exhausted, but wired, and can't decide what to ask them first, but decide I want to start with the hard stuff and get it out of the way.

"How many women have you fucked at the club?" I blurt out.

Simon freezes and stares at me from the kitchen where he's preparing a plate of snacks. Jude laughs as he enters from the bedroom, pulling a clean T-shirt over his head, then raking his fingers through his dark, wet hair.

"You don't waste time, do you?"

"It's a legitimate question, I think, all things considered."

"We'll stop doing scenes there if it bothers you," Simon says, walking over and setting a charcuterie board down on the coffee table in front of me. I reach out and grab a grape, popping it into my mouth.

"I didn't say that."

"It was implied," Jude says. "Why else would you lead with that?"

"We don't actually fuck anyone at the club, though," Simon says. "We're still in training."

"That's not to say we don't dole out lots and lots of orgasms." Jude grins over his wine glass.

I'm partly relieved, and more curious now about what exactly they do.

"So if you're more than just woodworking apprentices to Rick, what are you actually training to do?"

"It'd be clearer with a demonstration," Jude says. "But I don't think you have the energy for it."

"I'd give it a go," I say, though I'm really not interested in having to stand again, so if their demo requires me to use my legs, we're in trouble.

Simon shakes his head and settles on the edge of the coffee table facing me. "We don't have the right equipment up here anyway. It's what we wanted to show you tomorrow, when we have time and energy to focus on it."

"And before you get too antsy, we usually *don't* do scenes at the club. We've done exactly two, and the women were committed to other Doms. On loan, you could say. They volunteered and their Doms participated." He clears his throat. "Casey was one of them."

My stomach lurches, and I stop chewing the cracker I just put into my mouth and reach for my wine. I swallow my food in a lump and wash it down with a long swallow of alcohol.

"Okay," I say, not sure how I feel about this news.

"It was instructional. We needed a, um, live volunteer—preferably an experienced submissive. Rick and Max were there instructing us the entire time."

"Who was the other *volunteer*?"

"One of the other subs at the club. She's also *very* spoken for. She's got two lovers as well. One's a Dom, the other…" Jude looks at Simon. "What would you say Adam is?"

Simon snorts. "The best kind of deviant, because he let us use him as a guinea pig too, though we let Brit and Michael take over once we got him strapped in. He's a switch."

I'm too distracted to ask them to clarify what they're *strapping someone into* because I know that name.

I frown. "Who is Brit?"

"She's Casey's college roommate. At least she is now. I don't think they were when she started coming to the club."

I feel like I've fallen down a rabbit hole, because the Brit I knew was a friend at Stanford. I lost touch with her, but I know she was from New York, though she grew up in the City whereas I'm from the Lower Hudson Valley. Brit was always a quiet, graceful girl who hid a wickedly dark sense of humor behind her perfectly coiffed exterior.

I tilt my wine glass to my mouth, only to find it empty, so I hold it out. "I need more. In fact, why not open another bottle if you have it, because shit's getting way too weird tonight."

"Weird how?" Simon asks.

"Well," I say, accepting a refill when he tilts a freshly opened bottle over my glass. "I'm pretty sure I know Brit. Brittania Vale is her full name, isn't it?"

Two sets of eyebrows shoot up and the twins share a look. "How do you know?"

"Because she was at Stanford. We shared a few classes freshman year. She's from the City, so we had a lot in common. Then she transferred back here after some tragic accident that killed her mom. Now you're saying not only is she a member of Whitewood, but she's also Casey's roommate at Columbia? *And* you've probably seen her naked."

I take a long swallow from my glass that lasts until it's empty. I let out a soft belch, then hold the glass out for more. Simon narrows his eyes, but refills it anyway.

"That's all true," Jude says, a cautious note to his voice. "But it's much more complicated than that."

"No," Simon says. "It isn't complicated at all. Sarah, look at me." He sits on the edge of the coffee table facing me and gently extracts the wine glass from my hand. "What we do at the club is a *job*. We take it very seriously. Casey does too, and so do Max and Rick. It isn't about getting our rocks off with crazy orgies or anything. There are strict rules we always follow, and one of them is that no one lays a finger on anyone else without their explicit consent. When you walk into one of the rooms upstairs, you know what to expect."

"I think you're going to have to see it for yourself to get it," Jude says. "If you hadn't run away tonight, we would have showed you how things work."

"Just explain to me what you get paid to do, if it isn't sex. Because that's what Casey said she does there… gets paid to have sex while people watch. Is that what Brit does too?"

Simon takes a deep breath and lets it out slowly. "Yes, that's what Casey does with Max and Rick. Brit… they're more complicated. I think her Dom, Michael, is filthy rich, so they still pay for a VIP membership. Part of their kink is performing. They pretty much do whatever they want, while Casey's trio sticks to a choreographed routine, sort of like a Disney show."

I snort, because he did *not* just compare a sex show to the fucking Hoop Dee Doo Revue.

Jude snickers. "Okay, that's a bad analogy, but we're not a part of that. We don't have our own submissive. We don't perform. The only scenes we've been involved in were private. We're still learning, and the six of them have been happy to teach. What we actually do has evolved over the years. We started out as handymen, shadowing Rick and helping him fix things at the club. When he started teaching us how to fix some of the equipment, we started innovating and designing our own pieces. So what we do now mostly involves installing and testing new equipment. Casey, Brit, and their guys just help—they're our testers. We mostly watch and learn. The most contact we have with the girls is when we need to adjust straps and cuffs, and stuff like that."

I tilt my head, fixating on the way his mouth moves when he talks, because once he said "equipment," my mind went places I'm certain must be well beyond what he meant. One of the most vivid memories I have of our weekend alone was when they dug out some old toddler bouncy swings from the attic and turned them into a makeshift sex swing. We had *so* much fun with that, until one of the straps broke in the middle of one of our more enthusiastic rounds of sex. After that, they shoved the whole thing back into the box and into a dark corner behind my old baby clothes. It's probably still right where they left it.

"I want to see," I say, though I'm not sure my tongue is working. My head has gone fuzzy in the last few minutes, and all I can think about is being strapped into an adult version of that bouncy swing while the twins fuck me.

"Okay, I think you're done for the night," Jude says, peeling my fingers from around my wine glass and handing it to Simon.

"Show me the bouncy swing," I whine.

Simon chuckles. "I think you got through to her."

"Tomorrow, sweetheart. Right now, the only thing you need is to sleep off all that wine."

I reluctantly let them lead me to the bedroom, where Jude pulls me onto his lap in an armchair while Simon sets up a place for us to sleep. I'd happily crawl into one of their bunks, but that's not good enough for them.

I'm surprised when Simon pulls a large drawer out from beneath the bottom bunk and reveals a huge roll of foam. He proceeds to lay it out in the middle of the floor, then throws a set of sheets and several blankets on top. It's not the thickest mattress, but it's firm and sturdy, and more than enough to sleep on. The best part is that it's king-sized, so there's room for all three of us.

Simon grabs all the pillows off their beds and tosses them down, then I slide off Jude's lap and sprawl in the center of what now looks like a big nest on the floor. I'm drunk and happy, and let out a long sigh when they strip naked and join me beneath the blankets.

"We don't want anyone but you, Sarah. I hope you realize that," Simon whispers into my ear just before I drift off to sleep.

CHAPTER EIGHT

I'm drawn out of dreams into a hazy fog of pleasure. It still *feels* like a dream at first, so I surrender, because if it isn't real, I don't want to wake up. I'm on my stomach, and big hands caress my back, gliding down to my ass and back up. There are two sets, soon joined by two pairs of lips trailing kisses over my shoulders and down my spine.

My sleepy, hungover brain is slow to put the pieces together, but when it does—when it sinks in that this is all so very real—awareness cascades through me, magnifying the pleasure of their touch.

I let out a groan when one twin coasts his fingertips down the crease of my ass, parting my folds and sliding them into the wetness between my legs. He echoes the sound and bites down on my shoulder.

"Don't move, baby," Jude says. "I want you just like this."

I bite my lip and turn my head, finally opening my eyes. Simon's face greets me, his eyes bedroom-sleepy. His chin is propped on one hand, and he lightly caresses my face while his twin pushes my legs apart just a little. Jude's balls brush against my ass before his shaft slides down to notch at my core. I bite my lip, and it's all I can do to avoid lifting my hips to meet him.

Simon bends down and distracts me with a kiss just as Jude drives deep. I moan into Simon's mouth and clench my muscles tight around Jude's cock as he fucks me slow and hard. He braces one elbow at my side, curling his hand beneath my shoulder and holding on as he covers my body with his, his front to my back. My legs are barely spread enough to give him access, and the extra friction drives the pleasure higher.

"So tight. So perfect," he murmurs into my ear, grazing his lips across my jaw. I whimper and squirm, craving more contact to satisfy my rising need. Simon senses my desperation and pushes a hand beneath my belly to find my clit, but his teasing only makes it worse.

"She needs to come, brother," Simon says. "Hurry up."

Jude groans. "I'm close. Fuck, you feel good, Sarah."

He speeds up, every thrust taking me just to the edge of needing more. But despite it all, when Jude climaxes, I'm awash in a fresh blast of endorphins. He clutches my hand and bites down on my shoulder, gasping as his cock spasms inside me.

"Move your ass," Simon barks, pushing his twin to the side. A second later, he straddles my thighs and hauls my hips up. He spears me hard and fast, my pussy well-lubricated with his brother's semen and my own copious arousal. I gasp and groan, pushing back against his thrusts eagerly.

"I can't fucking get enough of you," he says, bending over my back to whisper in my ear. He snakes a hand around to find my clit again, fucking hard and fast while he teases me. Jude reclines at my side, giving me a lazy, sated smile and reaching out to play with my nipples one at a time.

"Come on Simon's cock, baby," he says. "Give it up for us."

I'm lost to the pleasure of their touch, their scent, of even being here in a bed with them. I'm that teenage girl again, exploring all the ways we can pleasure each other, all the ways our bodies can experience one another's. Except now there's no holding back; no fear or shame, just pure joy in rediscovering what we've lost.

I lose myself within a few more seconds, gaze latched onto Jude's. His eyes are bright with excitement and adoration when he watches me go over with his brother's cock slamming deep. Simon's climax follows a moment later and he huddles over me, arm wrapped around my torso while he nuzzles my neck.

We collapse in a heap a moment later. I laugh and bury my face in Simon's chest. "God, I forgot how amazing it felt being double-teamed by you two."

"We aim to please," Jude says. He heaves a sigh and hops to his knees, bending over to kiss me on the cheek. "You hungry? We can cook. Or if you're up for it, Rick and Max make a mean breakfast and are always happy for guests. Casey will probably be there."

"It still amazes me that you're friends with her now. The four of us never really interacted much as a group in high school."

"We barely knew you two before you graduated. You weren't even on our radar until your parents took us in," Jude says.

"Then you were *all* we thought about," Simon adds. "You were our entire world for those few weeks that summer. Sorry you and Casey lost touch."

Simon's belly gurgles loudly enough for me to hear. I pat it gently. "I take this as a hint that we should hunt down food.

I should check in with Casey anyway. Are you sure they don't mind us joining them?"

Jude rises and grabs his phone, then sends a quick text. A minute later, it buzzes with a reply. "We're on. Shower first?" He grins down at me.

"Yes, but just because we can all fit in there doesn't mean we should," Simon says. "If we want a *hot* breakfast, we need to get a move on."

They let me shower first, which I do quickly. Jude finds a spare unused toothbrush he lets me borrow, and I brush at one sink while he brushes at the other. Simon showers, then the twins trade places. It all feels so comfortably domestic, and I can't ignore a twinge of regret that I won't be able to stay. I don't want to dwell on that now, though; I have only a few weeks before I need to leave, so I plan to make it worthwhile.

My belly is in tangles when they lead me down the steps. I'm barefoot, wearing borrowed sweats and a tank top with my fancy bra underneath. No panties, since the ones I wore last night were appropriated and Jude isn't giving them up. But the path from their woodshop to the back door of the house is a quaint little flagstone trail, so shoes aren't required.

Before we even make it to the door, Casey bursts through with a huge grin and wide eyes. "Sarah! Oh my god, you have some *serious* explaining to do. How did I not know you and the twins were a thing? What the actual *fuck*? Get in here! I need to know everything!"

She grabs me by the arm and drags me through the door, laughing. I shoot an apologetic look back at Simon and Jude, and in the process catch Max's and Rick's amused glances as they sit at the kitchen table, watching my best friend haul me up the stairs to a bedroom and shut the door.

She parks me on the bed and plants her hands on her hips. "Okay, girl. Spill. Every. Fucking. Detail." She looks me over, frowning. "You want some clothes that fit?"

"Sure. Thanks. Um… where do I start?" She begins rummaging in a dresser that I recognize from her old house. Glancing around, I realize it's basically *her* old room, except in a different location. No evidence of a man in sight. "You don't share a room with them?"

"God, no. They're the worst cover hogs. Can you imagine trying to share a bed with two Doms? We each have our own room, but we have *our* room where we play when we're in the mood."

"I guess the twins are different," I muse.

Casey tosses a sports bra, some underwear, a pair of shorts, and a T-shirt my way, then heads to her closet, returning with a pair of cute thong sandals.

"Well, for starters, the twins aren't Doms." She plops down on the bed while I rise to change my clothes. "Unless they're different with you, anyway."

"They said they were in training. I thought that was what they meant."

"They're Rick's apprentices, but not for the dominance stuff. BDSM means different things to different people. Some are more into the BD side—bondage and discipline. Some into the DS—dominance and submission. Some are way into the S and M stuff. I don't think I've met many people at the club who love it all." She cocks her head and squints. "Well, maybe Adam, but he loves everything. The twins are really just all about the bondage. And the *devices*. Wait till they show you some of the stuff they've built."

"Sounds complicated."

She pats the bed, waving her hairbrush at me. "Sit. Let me braid your hair. It'll be like when we were kids."

I sit and close my eyes, relaxing as she works her expert fingers through the damp tangles in my hair. It feels just as easy and familiar being here with her as it felt sinking into a routine with the twins.

"I guess I just don't know enough about the whole scene. You probably know them better than I do, at this point."

"Not really. I know they were in the foster system. It didn't click that they were *your* foster brothers until I'd known them a while, but they didn't ever talk about you, so I didn't think anything of it. I just figured you weren't close."

I wince at that revelation.

"Sorry, did I pull your hair?" Casey asks, peeking at me in the mirror on top of her dresser just across from us.

"No. I keep getting reminded about how I fucked up, that's all. After you and I lost touch that summer after graduation, I connected with them. Like... *really* connected. Deeper than I have with anyone. Then everything went to shit, and I kind of ran away to college without really trying to reach out to them. It's no wonder they wanted to forget about me."

"I don't think they succeeded," she says. "If it's any consolation, they *always* seemed like they were holding out for something. Two of their hard limits at the club were kissing and fucking. They'd do just about everything else during training days. But the equipment they build is designed to be as hands-off as possible. It's a mind-fuck when you're strapped in."

"I don't even know what that means," I say, a queasy sensation filling my belly.

Casey snaps a tie around the end of the long French braid she put into my hair, draping the tail over my shoulder. She scoots close and wraps her arms around my waist, propping her chin on my shoulder.

"Sarah, honey, what they do at the club is business. They're professionals. Yes, they've seen me naked, but they've never laid a finger on me. Max and Rick are the only ones allowed to do that. If the twins have ever touched me, it was to make adjustments to the equipment while I was in it to make it safer for their paying clients. I guess I'm what you'd call their beta tester. But I imagine now that you're here, they'll prefer having you take over."

That makes me wince even harder. "That's the thing, Case —I'm *not here*. Not long-term. I'm going back to California at the end of August. Whatever this is, it's only temporary."

She narrows her eyes and smiles. "Well, then I guess they'd better take full advantage while they have you."

CHAPTER NINE

*D*espite the wild thoughts Casey's suggestion has put into my head, when we go down to breakfast, it feels as comfortable as my first morning home. Max and Simon tag-team our breakfast, which turns into a decadent spread with French toast, bacon, fresh fruit, and coffee. Rick breaks out a bottle of bubbly to celebrate my return, and we toast with mimosas in fancy glasses.

I feel like there's an elephant in the room, but the longer we spend together, the more I realize there are no secrets here. It's driven home when Rick praises the twins for an upgrade they made to some device that was integral to their show last night. I have no clue what a "gun machine bench" is, but I'm afraid to ask. Casey helpfully fills me in that it's like a mini pile-driver for getting fucked with a dildo, which leaves me blushing while the guys all grin at me.

"We can show you later," Jude offers.

"Which reminds me," Rick says, "how did the demo go last night? Did you land the client?"

Simon drops his fork. "Fuck!" My heart leaps into my

throat at the sudden shift in his mood. He shoves back from the table, grabbing his phone and jabbing at the screen.

Jude groans. "The fucking demo. I can't believe we forgot."

Rick's eyebrows rise and he glances between the twins, then smiles at me. "I guess you had a good reason."

"What happened?" I ask, not sure whether I should feel guilty for distracting them.

"We had an appointment to demonstrate our newest prototype for a venture capitalist who invests in kink-related products," Jude says. "They came in from out of town just for us."

"Well, they were new to Whitewood too," Max says. "So even if you didn't show, I guarantee they were entertained."

"That doesn't make me feel better." Jude stands and moves toward his brother, who's walking into the living room to make a call. He glances back at me, sees my stricken look, and pauses. "Sarah, I promise we have zero regrets about last night. I wouldn't change a thing. Though we may need to do a little damage control if we don't want to burn bridges."

"If I can help..." I begin, then stop, not sure I'm prepared to commit to something I know nothing about.

Jude bends to kiss me, then whispers in my ear, "You being here is more than we could ask for."

He joins Simon in the other room, and I'm too distracted to eat while we wait to hear the verdict. A few minutes later, the twins return, but their expressions are conflicted.

"Well, there's good news and bad news," Simon says. "The good news is that the company rep is here all weekend and is more than happy to see a demo tonight."

"The bad news," Jude says, "is that the Whitewood member we hired to help us demo the piece pulled a muscle at the gym this morning. She's out for at least two weeks."

They both glance at Casey, who shrugs. "You guys know we can't rework our show schedule on short notice. And I physically can't do more than one a night. Chloe wouldn't allow it, even if I had the stamina for it." She cocks her head to one side and looks at me, a devious smirk on her face. "Have you shown your toys to Sarah yet?"

My face flames and my eyes widen. "What the hell are you suggesting?"

"Absolutely not," Simon says. "This is *business*. Sarah's not ready for that, and even if she was, we wouldn't ask her to be put on display that way."

Now I stare at Simon. "Wait, I thought you wanted me to see what you were working on."

"I do. I'm just not about to ask you to help us demo the thing for an audience."

"I think she'd be great at it," Casey says. She leans closer to me with a wicked grin. "It's a mind-fuck the first time you do it while people are watching. *So hot.*"

As if they have a mind of their own, my nipples harden and tingle, and my pussy warms and throbs.

"Show me and let me decide for myself." I stare down both twins, who stare back with equally obstinate looks. I can tell they're about to wholeheartedly object to the idea when Max pushes his plate back and crosses his arms.

"Boys, remember to listen to your sub. The surest way to fuck things up is to be too rigid about your desires. In other words, if you love her, let her tell you what *her* limits are. Don't dictate them for her."

"What about *our* limits?" Jude asks.

Casey snorts. "Sounds like your only limit is jealousy, which does not make for healthy boundary-setting. Open your mind, dumbass."

"Nobody's going to be watching us now, are they?" I say.

"Let me experience it and tell you whether I'm okay with it. It might be fun."

I offer a hesitant smile because I'm completely in knots, my insides a confusion of curiosity, arousal, and abject terror. But this is something the twins love... something they want to make a career out of. I want to be able to share it with them at least once. I want a memory I can take away with me when I leave them again.

Jude takes my hand and pulls me out of my chair. "Well, we'd best get started then. If you're going to be our sub for this—and I'm not saying I'll agree to it—we need to get you up to speed fast."

"Good luck!" Casey calls after me as they lead me back out the door.

I follow the twins into the cool, concrete slab interior of the wood shop, and am immediately inundated with the scent of sawdust. It's calming at first, but when we head to a door at the far end of the space, a strange flutter takes residence in my belly. I remember this feeling... it's the same feeling I had the first day we were alone in the house. We'd already fooled around a little, but it was the first time we had complete freedom—the first time we could play in broad daylight.

I'm looking *forward* to whatever it is they have to show me, and I realize I don't really care how crazy it is. I *want this*.

Jude produces a key from his pocket and unlocks the door, leading me into a dark, windowless room. It smells different in here—more metallic, with a sharp aroma that isn't quite unpleasant, but not as comforting as the cut wood smell I'm used to. When Simon turns on the light, I understand why.

The room is entirely whitewashed concrete and cinderblock, with a big garage door at one end and wooden platform in the very center. On the platform is a contraption of polished metal and wood that looks more like an elaborate, futuristic sculpture than something functional. What I smell is the metal and whatever lubricant is used in the hydraulics for this... *device*.

"It's a time machine, isn't it?" I ask, stepping forward and staring up at the thing.

Jude chuckles. "If it was, we'd have already used it to go back and talk you into staying with us three years ago."

Their contraption is housed within a large, cubic framework, inside which is a sphere made of overlapping concentric circles of highly polished steel. It looks like a gyroscope, and when Jude taps on a small tablet screen attached to one post of the frame, the circles move, tilting and turning slowly and silently until they're aligned on a single vertical plane. In the very center of them is a harness made of wide straps covered in black satin.

"This is amazing. You guys built it? I suppose I was expecting some kind of wooden bench."

"We started with the usual BDSM toys—St. Andrews crosses and spanking benches. But we wanted to build something that was completely customizable based on the person or people using it. Jude programmed it, I designed it. We built it together." Simon tugs me up the step onto the platform and directs me to a circle of metal tile near the center, right in front of the harnesses.

"Stand here so we can get your measurements," he says.

I place my feet on the foot-shaped decals on the floor. "I feel like I'm about to get scanned by TSA."

"It's a little different. No X-rays involved." Simon stands in front of me, hands on my waist, and stares into my eyes. "You don't have to do this if you don't want to."

I smile up at him. "Are you kidding? You guys built *the*

ultimate adult bouncy swing. You're fucking insane if you think I don't want to try it out."

He lets out a relieved breath and smiles. "Then we need you naked."

He tugs at the hem of my shirt, and I raise my hands, letting him peel it off me. I kick off my sandals, then shimmy out of my shorts, standing still while both twins help pull my sports bra over my head and my borrowed panties down my legs. Jude gently nudges my ankles one by one for me to step out of my panties, then peers up at me as he coasts his hand back up my inner thigh. He lightly drifts his fingertips along my crease, just enough to tease—not to mention discover how very turned on I am already.

"I had a feeling you'd be into this," he says, standing and laying a searing kiss against my lips before moving away again.

Simon gathers my clothes and sets everything on a handy little shelf at one corner of the frame, then gestures at the floor again.

"Feet there. Arms straight out on either side, parallel to the floor, just like at the airport."

Jude returns to the small screen and taps it when I'm in position. A gust of cool air washes over me from the AC vent above us. It was starting to warm up, so I'm grateful for the cool air coming in. My heart is pounding as a series of red lights scan my body from multiple angles, and I glance around to see about half a dozen cameras trained on me from strategically located mounts.

"Are you recording this?"

"Every test is recorded. It's a safety protocol. We'll delete it afterward, if you're more comfortable. But the scans are to help us calibrate it for your frame. Once the measurements are dialed in, the device locks to your size and doesn't unlock until someone else is scanned. You can come see now."

Jude gestures, and I move to his side where a three-dimensional image of me is rotating in the center of his tablet screen. He taps a button that says "calibrate," and behind me, the device begins to whir and clink as pieces of it shift into position. The harnesses shake in the center while the cables attached to them lower and shorten, and the big circular hoops rotate, then pull apart.

"One last thing—we need your safe word." He taps another icon on the screen and an image of a microphone appears. "Lean close and say it. If you use it at any point during the scene, the device returns to neutral."

I lean in and say, "Starry Night," into the microphone, tilting my head to give Simon a sweet smile over my shoulder that he returns with a look brimming with affection.

"Okay, it's now or never," Simon says. "Ready to try out your own custom swing, Sarah?"

I'm so wet my thighs are slippery when I walk to the harnesses. When I get there, I see two more footprints just beneath them, closer together than the others. I pivot and stand in that spot, heart racing while the twins look on. Jude stares at me for a second, his fingers hovering over the tablet screen.

"Fuck me, I can't believe this is really happening right now. You're really *here*. This might be the best day of my life."

"Mine too," Simon says. He steps in front of me and crouches, then begins to attach each of the satin straps to my body. There are several for each leg, a hip harness, a vest-like harness, a few for each arm, and one final one that cradles my head and hooks into the vest.

When everything's hooked up, Simon stands back and looks me over. "Everything comfortable? Just so you know, the right wrist strap has a breakaway clasp so you can release yourself in case of emergency."

"I'm fine, but you look like you're about to explode." I smirk and drop my eyes to his crotch, which is bulging so prominently his jeans might be in danger of ripping. "Is there any rule that says you two need to have clothes on too?"

"I fucking love you," he says, stepping in close and grasping the back of my neck before he kisses me hard. I try to embrace him, but find myself restrained by the wrist straps. Hot arousal spikes through me at the realization that I am one hundred percent at their mercy now. The right cuff has a little give, but I don't pull harder. I want to do this right.

"Stand back, brother," Jude says. "Time for position one. Try to relax, Sarah. If you feel pain at any moment, tell us or use your safe word."

I don't know what "position one" means, but soon enough, I find out. The motors whir to life and the circles pivot. My limbs start to move like I'm a human marionette, shifting me into position. It's disorienting at first, then everything stops and I'm left suspended, arms tucked behind my back, in a seated position with my knees together, only my body is held up by nothing but the straps attached to my limbs.

That's when the floor opens up beneath me, but I can't see what appears, because my head is just as restrained as the rest of me. I can only look forward at the twins, who are taking their sweet time disrobing while *something* rises from below.

"Calibration is spot on," Simon comments, eyeing the tablet screen. "Nice work, brother."

"What is it?" I ask, making an effort to resist squirming.

Jude grins. "Something that'll make you feel really, *really* good."

CHAPTER TEN

My heart is pounding, but my attention is on the throbbing in my clit and the ache in my core that I get when I'm too aroused to think. Both twins are naked and hard, and I realize it's the first time I've seen them standing side by side when we weren't fully engaged. They are breathtaking like this, so breathtaking a deep flutter in my belly spurs the fervent wish that I didn't have to leave them again. But every thought disappears when something smooth and thick pushes at my wet folds.

Simon has the tablet in his hands now and taps the screen, then watches me intently. "Tell me what you think."

The object nudging at my opening rises again, slowly penetrating me from beneath. My mouth falls open because it's *thick*, stretching me until I gasp and heat floods my body.

"Too much?" Jude asks, taking a step closer.

I shake my head. "N-No. It's good, just... surprising. I like it."

He grins. "Just wait, it gets better."

"Oh god, you guys are trying to destroy me, aren't you?" I

try to smile, but wind up moaning as the slick object pushes even deeper. The texture feels like silicone, so I'm imagining some kind of big dildo, but it's also textured with little bumps that tease my G-spot as it enters me. I'm not prepared when it rises higher and another small protrusion works its way along the underside of my clit.

I gasp and clench at the handholds when the pressure sends a jolt of pleasure through me. But as if that isn't enough, the whole thing starts to *vibrate*.

I cry out, eyes widening. Simon's finger is on the tablet still, and he swipes. The vibration changes, and the whole thing begins to undulate inside me. I have a vibrator that's similar, but this is orders of magnitude more intense.

"Feel good?" Jude asks, his voice thick with need.

"Uh-huh," is all I can manage. I squirm, because it feels *so* good I want more.

He takes a step closer, then squats and peers beneath me. "Time to add the piston, I think."

"Got it," Simon says, then swipes on the tablet again.

The dildo slides down and out of me, and I moan in protest, but my moan turns into a grunt as the whole thing shoves back into me, then proceeds to piston in and out at a slow, steady pace. The protrusion that rubs my clit hits me exactly in the right spot each time, vibrating hard against my sensitive bundle. Pleasure rockets through me, and I grip the handholds hard.

"You're doing great, Sarah," Jude says from below. I glance down at him, but he's fixated on what's going on beneath me. He reaches out, and the next thing I feel are his fingers gently stroking around my filled opening, then gliding through my folds to the crack of my ass.

"Jude," I whine when he rubs a fingertip against my rear.

I'm perilously close to climax, and I'm going to lose it if he teases me just a little.

He stands and turns to Simon. "Time for a break, dude. Position two."

"On it."

The dildo abruptly disappears, but I'm too wound up to protest. The machine whirs to life again, lifting my arms above my head while my legs part. The machine keeps pulling until my inner thighs protest, and I worry for a second that it's not going to stop, but it does, just at the limit of comfort. My swollen pussy meets the cool air, and I sigh at the momentary reprieve, my pulse accelerating when Simon puts the tablet back into its dock and approaches.

Jude moves close behind me, nuzzling at the side of my throat as he wraps his arms around my middle. "You're amazing, Sarah."

"You guys are the amazing ones. I can't believe you *built* this thing."

He cups my bare breasts between the straps of the harness and thumbs my nipples. The sensation causes a fresh cascade of pleasure to run through me, down to my throbbing clit. I'm about to beg for more when Simon reaches me, dropping to his knees and leaning in. He extends his tongue and runs it up the length of my exposed pussy, stopping at my clit, which is a hard, swollen protrusion after all this stimulation.

He sucks it between his lips, rolling it against his tongue, and I buck and moan. He lets out a chuckle and pulls back, just looking at my naked flesh.

"You have *the* most gorgeous pussy. Your clit's like sucking on a cherry. Do you know that?" He parts my folds with one hand while teasing the fingers of his other up and down my soaked skin.

I groan. "I know I have a lot going on down there."

I'm honestly self-conscious about how *generous* my pussy is. I have full, fat lips, inner labia that protrude, and a clit that gets so big there's no way a guy can't find it when I'm turned on. It's earned me some odd looks from both men and women who have seen me naked. But I've never felt self-conscious about it with the twins.

Jude hums against my ear, still toying with my nipples. "I bet it's why you're so damn responsive."

"I'm glad you enjoy all my assets. But I have a question."

Simon tilts his head back to look at me. "What's that?"

"Are you going to actually fuck me? Because I really, *really* need to be fucked."

Both twins laugh and Simon stands, leaning in to press his forehead against mine. "What did you think we paused for? I just wanted to admire our creation for a moment—you strapped in and spread out for us. We could do whatever we wanted with you right now. But I have a feeling you'd love just about anything we did, wouldn't you?"

"As long as it's not just talking about what you're going to do," I say.

Jude's hands disappear from my breasts and his warmth fades from my back. A second later, I feel his tongue teasing between my legs from behind, hooking into my vagina before gliding back to my ass. I gasp, then bite my lip and hold my breath when his fingers, now coated in something cool and slick, press against my rear opening. He pushes one finger into me, and Simon devours my moan as his brother invades my ass.

"Are you ready for me, Sarah?" Jude rumbles. Simon leans back and gazes into my eyes, one hand clutching my jaw while he toys with my nipples. He grazes his thumb over my lips and I open, allowing him to slip the digit inside for me to suck. His eyes are dark pools of desire, and I nod slightly at the question in them.

"She's ready," he says in a low voice, keeping his gaze fixed on my face as his brother removes his fingers from me and closes in against my back. Jude presses his thick cockhead to my ass, and I let my eyes fall closed, forcing my body to relax for the thick shaft he's about to penetrate me with.

We discovered the joys of anal sex together when we were younger. They'd wanted to try it, but I'd refused to let them play with me until after they'd both seen what it felt like for themselves. This resulted in the three of us locked in the bathroom with a bottle of baby oil, coating our fingers and sliding them into ourselves, reporting what we felt. They both enjoyed it, but not nearly as much as they enjoyed fingering *me* once I gave the go-ahead. Then, of course, fucking me.

Being suspended and restrained so both of them have easy access to everything only magnifies the pleasure when Jude pushes his cock into my ass. Simon cradles my head, kissing me slowly until Jude starts to thrust. Then he presses his own hot tip to my entrance and slides in.

It's more amazing than I could have imagined, being turned into their plaything. They bracket my suspended body, Jude cupping my breasts, his teeth buried in my shoulder while he thrusts deep into my ass. Simon curls his hands around to grip my cheeks, spreading them even wider for his twin. He kisses me the entire time, and his kisses are so delicious they're almost better than their cocks driving into me over and over. It's as if the sex itself isn't close to enough for him; he needs to be connected to me on an even deeper level, and I feel exactly the same.

The fluttering in my belly intensifies, and when I climax, it overwhelms me. Tears are streaming down my face by the time the twins finish. Simon makes a hum of concern against my mouth as he pulls out and frowns at me.

"Did we hurt you? Sarah, why are you crying?"

"Because I love you both so much it hurts. And because I'm going to have to leave you again, and it's going to destroy me."

CHAPTER ELEVEN

"Take her down, now," Jude commands. He moves away so fast I let out a whimper of protest, but he's back within seconds, buttoning his jeans, then hurriedly unstrapping one side of my body while Simon takes care of the other. The next thing I know, he's lifting and carrying me to the edge of the platform, where he sits and cradles me on his lap.

Simon joins us after putting on pants. He pulls my legs across his thighs and gives me an earnest look. "Tell me what you meant, Sarah. Why do you have to leave?"

"Because I have a *life* in California. I have to finish college. I have a career lined up when I do. I can't just drop it after working so hard."

"We wouldn't ask you to give anything up for us. You know that," Jude says, sounding offended.

"I know, which is why this is so hard." I rest my palm against his cheek. "I didn't expect to see you two this summer. I thought I'd just spend a few weeks visiting my parents and then go back. But now all I want is to stay, even though I know it's a dumb idea."

"I don't know about that…" Simon starts, but cuts himself off when Jude shoots him a withering look. He sighs. "When do you leave?"

"I only took three weeks off from my internship. I can't extend it without looking like a flake, and this internship is key to earning a position when I graduate. It's a really good starting salary, even for California. But now…" My eyes start to burn again, and I reach out and clutch Simon's hand as the words get trapped in my throat. "The idea of leaving you…"

"Shh," Jude says, squeezing me tighter and nuzzling my cheek. "We'll figure it out. If nothing else, we know we need to make the most of the time we have, right?"

"I don't want to lose you guys again."

Simon moves around to crouch in front of us, lifting both hands to cup my face so I have no choice but to look at him. "You won't. No matter what happens, I can promise you that much. You will *never* lose us. We'll work it out. I promise."

"It was the machine, wasn't it?" Jude says in a subdued voice.

I stare at him, confused until I see a slight curl at the corner of his mouth and a twinkle in his eye. I laugh. "Yes, your amazing, ingenious sex machine made me fall completely and irrevocably in love with you."

"Wait till you see Position Three." He waggles his eyebrows at me.

I glance over his shoulder at the inert contraption, the straps dangling loose. "Guys, this is big. I can't believe you blew off an investor last night just to spend time with me. I mean, this is the kind of thing that could make your entire careers. It's… beyond words, how clever it is."

"You inspired us—I hope you know that. All those experiments we tried when we were younger stuck with us." Simon hops up and grabs the tablet from its bracket again. He taps the screen, and the straps retract on their wires while the big metal circles whir back into their neutral positions.

"I want to help. Is the guy supposed to come here to, um, watch?" My face heats at the prospect of repeating today's adventure in front of an audience. Then my eyes widen and I ask, "It *is* a guy, right? Or is the investor a woman?" I don't know why, but somehow that would make it harder.

Simon inspects the equipment, then heads back to sit beside me. "The investor's name is Sheridan Keene. He flew out from LA just to see this thing, so we're pretty lucky he was laidback about being stood up. I guess Chloe did a little entertaining on our behalf and convinced him we'd make it up to him."

Jude squeezes my thigh. "And no, he's not coming here. This is our prototype. We built a second model for Whitewood that's locked in a room at the club now. Chloe was our initial investor. She plans to charge a premium to let people use it, but no one's allowed in the room unless we're there. We'll need to train a couple more staff as operators. They can then train any Doms who want to use it."

"How many other people will be there?" I ask, suddenly uncertain about going through with this, even though I want to help.

"Just him. Unless you want a bigger audience."

I let out a breath. "Good. No. I just thought because of how Casey described what she does that *watching* was, you know, how things are done there."

"Oh, right. You haven't actually been upstairs yet, have you?" Simon says. "Well, that's definitely something we'll need to remedy. We'll head over early so you can see the place with fewer members present. Let's head upstairs and get cleaned up for now." He stands and reaches out to pull me to my feet.

"I should actually head home for a bit first. I need to face the parents at some point," I say as I follow them both up the back staircase into their apartment.

"Do you want us with you?" Simon asks.

"Yeah, we're totally there if you need us," Jude adds.

Their eagerness to have my back makes me smile, but I shake my head. "No. At least not today. Let me ease them into the idea first. Maybe before I go back to California, you can come over for dinner or something, though."

I gather my things and bid them both farewell, a fresh surge of anxiety filling me as I back out of the driveway. It's not about them, though, or the favor I agreed to do for them tonight. This time, it's all about facing my parents about the twins.

It's a normal lazy Saturday at the Nolan house. My sisters are still parked in front of the TV in the den, watching cartoons, when I walk in. They greet me with chirpy hellos. I wave back.

"Sarah, is that you?" Mom calls from the kitchen.

"Yep!" I wander in, toss my things onto one of the barstools, and sit on another. She's up to her elbows in bread dough while Dad sits at the kitchen table in the sunny nook, staring at his laptop.

"How was your night out with Casey?" She gives me a cautious look, making me wonder why she doesn't mention the twins. My text to my folks last night was pretty clear about where I would be.

"It was… good. Better than I expected, to be honest." I briefly contemplate spilling every detail, including where we went, but decide now isn't the time to tell my parents about the kinky sex club. It's unlikely there will ever be a good time for that. But there is one detail I need to make sure is out in the open, since she's obviously not going to bring it up.

"That's wonderful. I'm so glad you two reconnected. I never quite understood what happened between you."

"It's complicated. A lot happened that summer after we graduated."

Mom pauses her kneading and looks up at me. A stray curl of her graying brown hair flutters across her face, and she blows it off. She studies me for a second, then nods and looks down at her hands.

"I think about that summer a lot, you know. Sometimes I wonder if we overreacted. But you were so young. And you know behavior like that can risk our foster care license."

"I was eighteen, and the twins still needed a home. We could have worked it out."

Mom winces and glances at Dad, who closes his laptop and props his arms on the table, looking at us both. "The twins left without a goodbye, Sarah—you know that as well as I do. But if it makes you feel better, they didn't go far. Rick Bennett took them in—" He trails off when I lift an eyebrow at him, then chuckles. "But you probably figured that out already."

Still, the fact that Dad chose to tell me this takes me a moment to process. "You knew where they were all this time?"

He presses his lips into a tight line and lets a long breath out through his nose. "I think a lot of bad decisions were made that summer. I'm not blameless, either. And for the record, I *don't* think what you and the twins did was one of them… as long as you were safe, that is, and the fact that I'm not a grandfather is enough proof of that. But emotions were high at the time. I didn't really cool off until you left for college. By that time, I just thought it was better to leave things alone. You were moving on—all three of you. If it was meant to be, well… I don't blame you for wanting a reunion. I just hope it lived up to your expectations."

"Dad…" I'm speechless as I stare at him, stunned at the completely unexpected confession. After a moment, I manage to gather my thoughts and clear my throat. "Actually, it was pretty amazing. Better than I could have expected. They're doing well, and I'm hoping to spend a lot more time with them while I'm here. So fair warning, but I probably won't be around much."

Mom makes an odd sound, and my dad chuckles. I look at Mom, who rolls her eyes. "You couldn't just pick one, could you? You had to have them both."

Before I can answer, Dad rises and moves to her side, pulling her against him. "We could never choose just one kid, Sheen. We fell in love with just about every wayward child we fostered. I was growing to love the twins too. They're good boys. The way I figure, Sarah's love just evolved at a time in her life when other things were evolving too."

My eyes burn with tears, and I reach for a tissue from the box at the end of the counter. "You guys are literally *the* best parents. I'm so sorry I haven't been home all this time."

"Oh, honey," Mom says, reaching across the bar to caress my cheek with a floury hand. "We knew you'd come home when you were ready. And please tell Jude and Simon that they can come home too."

PART III
ALL IN

CHAPTER TWELVE

Whitewood is like a different place when we arrive in the early evening. There are people there, but they're in more causal outfits, and the atmosphere is more relaxed and informal. I follow the twins into the foyer, where Chloe greets us with a warm smile.

"I'm so glad you decided to return, Sarah."

My cheeks heat, and I nod. "I'm sorry about last night. I was just so surprised to see the twins again. I guess I didn't react well."

"It's important that everyone's comfortable when they're here. Please don't hesitate to call a timeout whenever you need. You're not obligated to stay if you're unhappy."

"Thank you, but I really am curious. And since Jude and Simon asked me to help them with their meeting this evening, I thought I ought to get acquainted with the place."

Chloe raises both eyebrows and glances at the twins. "Are you sure she's ready?"

"It's a private show, and we'll be there to coach her through it," Jude says, resting his hand against my lower back.

Looking at me again, she asks, "You've seen their machine, right?"

Oddly, this question doesn't embarrass me. I share a knowing look with Jude and Simon. Simon nods and smiles.

"The machine wouldn't exist if not for Sarah, actually. It was made for her."

The confession seems to please Chloe, and she waves us farther in. "You three enjoy your evening. Good luck tonight."

I have butterflies in my belly when the twins lead me to an antique elevator that takes us to the second floor. We're greeted by a gorgeous, curvaceous woman named Olivia, who looks like a pin-up model wearing satin lingerie. She explains the Whitewood rules and shows me a colorful list of kinks that resembles a fancy restaurant menu.

"Sarah's sticking with us tonight, so we can skip the bands. We have a private meeting."

Olivia glances at me with eyebrows raised. I shake my head. "I want the full experience. I think that means I should wear a white velvet band and a dark gray band on my right arm, right?"

"She's paying attention," Olivia says with a nod of approval. "You two shouldn't let her out of your sight, if you want to hold onto her. Here, let me get you all set up."

She grabs three ribbons of each color, then rounds the counter to affix each one to our arms. Mine go on my right arm and the twins' go on their left arms, the different sides signifying givers versus receivers of the designated kinks. White means we're giving a show. Gray means we're into bondage.

"They should come up with a new color for sex machines," I suggest as Olivia finishes securing my ribbon. "Silver lamé, maybe?"

Olivia shakes her head. "That color's for celebrities and star-fuckers. But maybe something striped. I'll have to see what I can come up with."

"Sheridan Keene should be arriving in about an hour. Can you direct him to the private suite when he gets here?" Simon says.

"You got it." Olivia gives us a little wave as we head to the right, down one wing of the second floor.

The hallway is lined with elaborately framed windows that display closed curtains on the opposite side. Three men and a pair of women are gathered by one, chatting like old friends about mundane topics. It's all so *normal* and unassuming, it's easy to relax.

One of the women smiles brightly at me. "A new face! Welcome to Whitewood. You're just in time to see one of the best shows here."

My heartbeat stutters and I glance at the wide, curtained window, then at the twins. "Can we watch?"

"If you want. Just... don't run away, okay?" Simon says.

"Why would I run away?"

The curtains start to move, and sultry, bump-and-grind music begins to play. Jude tilts his chin at the window and slips closer, hooking his hand around my waist. Simon takes up position on my other side, as if they're guarding me with their bodies, or making sure they can trap me from running away again. But I am committed, at least for the rest of my visit.

Then I catch the eye of the girl on the other side of the glass, and my eyes widen. It's Casey.

"Holy shit!"

"Are you okay with this?" Jude asks.

"Are you kidding? I *have* to see it now."

I take a step closer, and Casey grins and waves. Max and

Rick appear from the shadows, wearing nothing but tattered jeans and looking sexy as hell, their shirtless torsos glistening.

Rick glances toward the window and smiles, then shakes his head, saying something I can't hear. Casey bounces a little, her full breasts jiggling in the tiny baby-doll negligée she's wearing. Rick nods at Max, who grabs the hem of Casey's outfit and pulls it over her head, then squats in front of her and slowly slides her panties down her thighs.

When she's naked, they pause, and each man kisses her. Then Max takes hold of Casey's arms and pulls her wrists together in front of her.

The pair proceed to spend the next ten minutes slowly trussing up my friend with bright red ropes. The bindings remind me of the positions I was moved into by the machine, except every movement of Casey's limbs is determined by the ropes Rick carefully knots around parts of her body.

"That's a work of art," I say when they pause and step aside so we can see the results. Casey's hands are crossed over her midsection, and a webwork of perfectly knotted ropes cover much of her torso, leaving just enough space for her breasts to emerge. Rick completes the work by securing one of her legs, her knee bent and suspended from a rope anchored to the ceiling. Her other leg hangs down, toe pointed and brushing the floor. She looks like a dancer caught in a spider web.

Rick reaches up and spins her slowly. Above her, I see the pivoting anchor point where the ropes originate, designed so they can turn her for maximum effect.

When she faces away, Max moves to her other side. I can't see what he does, but she drops her head back, her long hair skimming the ropes crisscrossing her back.

Then Max drops to his knees, and it's obvious he's licking

her exposed pussy. My core heats as I watch. I can't tear my eyes away.

Rick turns Casey ninety degrees and kneels as well, taking his turn attending to her. Even though she's bound and at their mercy, it's more like she's their goddess and they want nothing more than to worship her body.

After a moment, Rick stands and turns her again. This time Max comes around and kneels, his back to us, returning his mouth to her core. Casey's eyes are closed and her head tilted back. Rick moves behind her and gathers her hair in one fist, pulling her back a little farther. He whispers something in her ear, and she tries to nod. He glances at the audience as he grazes his palm over her jaw and throat, curling his fingers around her neck. It's an act of utter dominance, and I'm enthralled by my friend's submission. The display is brief, but powerful. Then Rick carefully begins to plait her hair, taking another length of red rope and weaving it around the entirety of her long braid.

The effect is stunning when they stand back for a second, letting the watchers simply take in the bound woman in the center of the room.

"Are they going to fuck her?" I ask under my breath.

"Not until the end," a woman says. She eyes both the twins with interest, catching sight of their arm bands, then mine. She's wearing a gray ribbon as well, but thankfully catches on to the fact I'm with them and doesn't make any overtures, though it's clear she's thinking *something* of the sort.

"It's a two-hour show. Then they take a break."

When I look through the window again, Casey's in an entirely different position. She's hovering parallel to the floor, facing down, with Rick carefully knotting the ropes above her. Both her knees are bent now, heels nearly touching her ass, her legs splayed wide and her arms behind her back. It's like a dance, watching them move, spin her around, then tease her exposed flesh.

Max crouches beneath her, kisses her on the mouth, then proceeds to suck on one of her nipples while he teases the other. Rick steps away to a cabinet and returns with a pair of toys and a bottle of lube. He coats one of the toys and spreads Casey's cheeks, then gently inserts it into her ass. I can just see a side view of her face, and she's biting her lip, cheeks flushed. The idea of being bound like that is incredibly arousing, and my core aches at the thought of what's in store for me later.

Rick holds up the other toy for the viewers to see. It's a small, silver, egg-shaped vibrator that he pushes inside Casey's vagina, then grins when he presses a button on a corresponding remote. The way she jerks and moans gives away the fact that he just turned it on.

My insides feel wound up tight, watching her squirm and twist, her movements causing her to rotate. When her backside faces us, we have a clear view of her soaked pussy and the plug buried in her ass. Her flesh is engorged and glistening, fluid nearly dripping out of her.

Rick grabs one of her ass cheeks and squeezes, then twists the plug, pulling it out, then pushing it back in. Her legs strain against the ropes and her hips rock. Max steps to her other side, halting the rotation, and then nods at Rick, who produces the remote control from his pocket and hits another button.

A cry reaches my ears, followed by Casey cursing. Max grabs hold of the plug in her ass and starts to fuck her with it while Rick slides his fingers between her thighs and finds her clit, rubbing it quickly. His lips move, and it looks like he's counting down. When he gets to one, Casey writhes and bucks, her orgasmic wails audible through the window. It goes on for about a minute before she falls limp. The entire time, my eyes are fixed between her spread thighs, my own core clenching and releasing in sympathy.

The guys step to the side then, leaving her hanging there with the toys buried inside her. I can hear her begging as her Doms pull up chairs and sit. They're both obviously aroused, yet don't seem too fazed by the enormous bulges in their pants. Rick hits a button on the remote again, and Casey relaxes.

"Are they going to leave her hanging like that?"

"Just for a little while. They have to give her time to recover. Act Two is much more acrobatic," the woman says, smiling at me.

"We should head to the suite," Jude suggests. "I want to make sure Sarah's relaxed and ready when Sheridan arrives."

"I'm kind of ready now," I say, because after seeing just a piece of Casey's show, I don't think I care if anyone's going to watch. I really need to be fucked.

Jude grins. "I'm not surprised. But we're going to take this slowly. I want you ready to explode when he's watching, not before."

"So you're going to torture me, is what you're saying."

"Remember your safe word," Simon replies.

CHAPTER THIRTEEN

*D*espite my conviction that I won't really need it, I repeat "Starry Night" over and over in my head as the twins lead me to another wing of the mansion. The music piped into this area has a more subdued techno-dance theme that settles in my belly when we reach a glossy black door. There's no big window looking into this room, and the knob has a shiny keycode entry pad at the top.

Jude taps in a code, and the lock disengages. He pushes the door open, and Simon grabs my hand, pulling me through when his twin steps aside to hold the door for us.

This machine is identical to the one in their shop, but the difference between the rooms is like night and day. This one is decorated in the style of a luxurious lounge, with dark silk damask wallpaper covering all but one wall, which is entirely paneled in mirrors. On the floor just past the threshold is an elaborate Turkish carpet that covers half the room, but the machine itself rests on an ebony wood floor, its platform just as polished as the floor.

Jude closes the door behind us and heads to the back corner, where he opens a hidden panel in the wall. The lights above us begin to shift on their tracks and move into new positions, spotlighting the machine. My palms have started to sweat, but I'm more excited than nervous.

Simon darts a hungry look my way and squeezes my hand. "It's going to be so hard to take this slow."

"Do you regret asking me to do this?" I ask.

"Not for a second. It's a fantasy come true."

"More so than what we already did?"

He lifts one shoulder and smiles. "Setting is everything, I guess. Back at the shop, it was more like when we were kids playing around, you know? Here it feels ... official."

"Like I'm really your submissive?"

He leads me to a door in the back of the room. "It isn't like that for us. It isn't about dominance; it's about experimentation. We just want to play with the giant toy we built. The only reason we tie you up is because that's how it works. That's not to say it can't be used by a Dom and a sub, but that's not really what we get out of it." He turns to me and his brows crease. "Unless that's what you want...?"

I shake my head and laugh nervously. "No. I guess I'm still trying to wrap my head around it all. I'm all over the whole *toy* angle, though. I love toys. Would it be weird if I told you I have kind of a big collection of them back in California? I've tried out pretty much anything I could use on myself. I think I scared away a couple guys when I tried sharing with them."

He gives me a wicked smirk and moves to stand in front of me. "They weren't prepared for what a deviant you are, were they?" He lifts a hand and brushes my hair away from my cheek, his eyes sparkling with amusement. "I'd love to see all your toys sometime, Sarah. I know for a fact there's nothing you could show me that would make me run."

I search his gaze for any hint of hesitance at getting that close again, now that he knows my time here is limited. It hadn't occurred to me until now that they could come visit, though, and it sounds like that's what he's promising.

"I would love that," I say.

"But first, we need to get you ready for tonight."

He steps away, and I take in the rest of the room, which is a large dressing room that opens into a spacious, marble-tiled bathroom. He opens a mahogany wardrobe and retrieves a black silk robe and a couple of bottles, tossing one of the bottles past me. I glance over my shoulder just as Jude catches it and slips up beside me with a grin.

"This is my favorite part," he says.

"What part is that?"

Simon sets the bottle on a dressing table and drops to a squat, reaching up to unfasten the button on my shorts. "Getting you naked and oiling you up."

Jude tugs at the hem of my tank top, and I let him peel it off, then divest me of my bra. He carefully removes the ribbons from my arm, then begins gathering my hair and braiding it. When he's finished, he drapes the long plait over my shoulder, and I see that he wove my ribbons into the strands.

Once I'm undressed, they both strip and slip into silk pajama bottoms, then flip the caps on the little bottles and squirt golden oil into their palms.

Their hands are warm and slick as they smooth the oil over my skin. Simon begins at my feet, working his way carefully up each leg while Jude starts at my shoulders and back, working his way down.

Simply having their hands on me like this is enough to make me hot, and my nipples are pebbled peaks, even though Simon does no more than swipe his palms over them to coat them in the fragrant, glistening liquid.

Jude's phone buzzes from inside his discarded pants

pocket, and he quickly wipes his hands on a towel before retrieving it and tapping the screen.

"Sheridan's here. Olivia just sent him our way. I'll go meet him," he says, then kisses me on the cheek. "You're going to be *amazing*, Sarah."

My knees are a little weak with both arousal and nerves. I take a deep breath, and it comes out as a shaky sigh. Simon slides his oiled palms back down to my hips and stares up at me from where he's still crouched.

"You okay?" he asks, rising to his feet.

"Just nervous. Have you met this guy? What's he like?"

"He's a pro. Based on our research, he only invests in top-notch equipment—stuff rich kinksters are willing to pay a pretty penny for."

"No, I mean, what's he *like?* As a person. He's going to be watching me… us. Is he going to want to, you know, sample the goods?"

Simon's eyebrows shoot up and he glances toward the door. He clears his throat. "Um, we've chatted with him on video conferences a few times, when we first showed him the machine. He's British. In his late thirties, I think, maybe forty. He's rich and good-looking. No idea how tall he is, but I guess he looks a little like that blond guy from *Game of Thrones*. He's not some old, creepy pervert, if that's what you're worried about. Everything's above board. Sampling the merchandise, though… that wasn't something we discussed. He's here to see the machine. Not you."

I nod, but now I'm picturing some hot celebrity watching me and the twins having sex, and I'm not sure whether I like the idea. First of all, how can he stand it, if he's at all good at his job?

"Sarah, what's cooking in that head of yours?"

"Just that it must be a really frustrating job, if all he does is watch other people demo their toys."

He narrows his eyes. "True, but like I said, he's a pro. And you also know we have strict rules at the club so that no one has to do anything they don't want to do. You already agreed to let him watch, but he won't touch you. Not unless you want him to."

"Is... Is that even an option? I mean, I don't want to do it if you guys wouldn't like it, but if I decided I'd be into it, and if he wants to, can we try it out?"

Simon studies me for several beats, and I stare into his eyes, determined not to reveal the complete uncertainty I feel about what I just suggested. When he slowly nods, my heart rate skyrockets. "We can check in with Jude when he returns with Sheridan. If we're all on board with the idea—and more importantly, if our guest is too—I'm game to add him to the mix."

"Is it crazy to ask, not having met him at all? And after reconnecting with you two... I don't want to ruin what we have either."

"Nothing at Whitewood is crazy, Sarah. You know us. Jude and I are both just as open to experimentation as we ever were. Trying new things is kind of *our* kink. So if you're into the idea of getting railed by three guys while strapped into a machine, honestly, that's pretty fucking hot.

"And Sheridan's one of us. Jude and I both like him enough to do business with him. Max and Rick helped us vet him, and they trust him too. Rick's licensed a few of his own designs to Sheridan's company."

I heave a breath and Simon chuckles, then kisses me. "Baby, you never have to be afraid to ask for what you want, but let's meet him before we decide, okay?"

I nod, then slip my arms into the robe he holds up for me

and tie the belt at my waist. I'm so aroused it isn't funny, so I hope actually meeting this guy doesn't become a huge turn-off.

We step out the door just as Jude enters the room, followed closely by a tall, broad-shouldered man in a sharp suit. He's slightly taller than Jude, but not by much, and he only vaguely resembles the actor Simon compared him to—he's about ten years younger and ten times as attractive.

Simon whispers, "Wait right here," and leaves me standing beside the machine while he goes to greet the new arrival.

"Sheridan Keene, this is my brother, Simon," Jude says.

"We're sorry we had to postpone the demo," Simon says, shaking Sheridan's hand. "Thank you so much for being flexible."

"I'm nothing if not accommodating," Sheridan says with a warm smile, his accent not nearly as pronounced as I'd expected. It's as refined as his good looks. "I was well taken care of here. And your brother filled me in on why you missed our appointment last night. I completely understand."

His easy manner allows me to relax just a little, but when his gaze shifts to me, I tense again.

"This must be Sarah." He strides over and stops in front of me, holding out his hand. "A pleasure. I don't begrudge the twins the need to prioritize your reunion. I see why they did."

I stumble over a thank-you as I offer my hand. Rather than simply shake it, he bends and brushes his lips over my knuckles. A waft of pleasant-smelling aftershave reaches my nose as I stare at the top of his head, which is covered in dark blond hair that looks smooth and fine as silk.

Simon catches my eye, one brow raised, and I smile, positive the heat in my cheeks is enough to tell him that yes, I'm interested in following through with my suggestion.

"Sarah's more than her looks," Jude says. "But you'll have a chance to observe just how special she is soon."

Sheridan straightens and steps back a pace, nodding, then looking around the room. A big, comfortable armchair rests off to one side, arranged with a view of the machine. On a table beside it is a bucket containing a bottle of champagne and four glasses.

"I believe this is my spot," he says, striding over to the chair. He lifts the bottle and inspects it, then nods. "May I pour you three a glass?"

"I'm good," I say, and the twins both decline as well. Sheridan pours himself a flute of the bubbly liquid, then sits and crosses one ankle over his knee.

"Then I am ready when you are. As excited as I am to be here, there is no rush. My goal is to see the machine in action, nothing more or less. If there's anything you need from me, you need only ask. I might ask questions, but otherwise, pretend I'm not here."

"You ready?" Jude asks softly, an eager gleam in his eyes.

"Yes, except…" I give Simon a beseeching look. He clears his throat.

"Let's get you strapped in," he says, tilting his head toward the machine. Jude frowns at him, then follows as Simon leads me up the short steps onto the center of the platform, where we're out of earshot of Sheridan if we whisper.

They both block me from Sheridan's view. Jude squeezes my arm. "If you need to back out, say so now. We won't blame you."

"It isn't about that, is it?" Simon asks.

I shake my head and look at Jude. "I told Simon I might want to let Sheridan, um, *participate*. If neither of you object, I think it could be fun—if he's into it, anyway. I wasn't sure at first, but now that I've met him…" I shrug.

Jude glances over his shoulder, then looks at his brother. "You'd be cool with this? He's only wearing a voyeur ribbon; he really only came to watch today. Chloe said last night he did a lot more than watch, though. He's pretty hardcore, but he followed the rules, so she approved his membership here."

"Can't hurt to ask," Simon says. "But we can wait for the right time. Are you ready to get strapped in?"

He toys with the tie to my robe, and Jude steps to a small plinth at the edge of the platform where the tablet that controls the machine rests. When Simon tugs the end of the tie and my robe falls open, I can't help but shift my gaze to Sheridan.

He looks completely relaxed and in his element, sitting back in the big chair with the crystal champagne flute in his hand. But when Simon pushes the robe off my shoulders, Sheridan's eyes blaze. I take a breath and force myself to look at Simon.

He smiles. "Poor guy won't know what hit him, once he has a taste of you."

CHAPTER FOURTEEN

Jude mans the controls while Simon straps me in, just like this morning. Except unlike this morning, we have an audience.

Sheridan sips his drink while he watches, and I can't help but look his way every few seconds while Simon secures the body harness and each of the buckled bands in a dozen strategic locations. I feel even more exposed than before, but it's thrilling, and when Simon pauses to check in, I can't help but let out a giddy laugh.

"I can't believe I'm doing this," I whisper.

"You are meant for this," Simon whispers back.

I'm in the second position they had me in this morning, the straps supporting me as if I'm seated in a swing, my knees spread wide and my arms raised. He tests the tightness of the harness that crisscrosses over my midsection, then the sections that encompass my groin. They're no more than a pair of wide loops with a little more give than the other straps to allow for flexion. But when Simon slips his fingers between the strap and my flesh, he keeps going until his knuckles graze my bare core.

When he encounters how very turned on I am, he takes a deep breath and drops his gaze between my thighs. "This only proves my point." He withdraws his fingers from beneath the strap and lightly coasts a fingertip over the upper ridge of my exposed clit, which pokes out from beneath its hood like the shining pistil of a flower. He applies only slight pressure, but it's enough to make me gasp.

I peek past his shoulder at Sheridan. Is he turned on watching this? What if he's so desensitized to this kind of thing that it doesn't even affect him?

Sheridan's eyes meet mine, and he licks his lips and smiles. "Looks amazing so far. May I see her?"

Simon steps to the side and faces him. "The straps are nylon encased in a thin layer of high-tech foam and wrapped in cotton microfiber for comfort. The closures are steel with breakaway capability. Everything's been thoroughly tested for safety."

Sheridan nods, his gaze fixed on my exposed pussy. God, I hope he isn't thinking I'm some kind of mutant because of how swollen my clit gets when I'm turned on. But he doesn't look disgusted by me. On the contrary, he looks distracted. That's when I notice the prominent bulge in his pants and can't help but smile.

Simon nods to Jude, who taps the tablet's screen. The giant rings of the machine shift, moving my limbs until I'm in a standing position with my hands at my sides. I have just enough slack to swing my arms a little.

Sheridan tuts. "I liked the other position better. How many are there to choose from?"

"There are over three hundred configurations loaded into the program," Jude says. "Obviously there can be infinite configurations, but most of them aren't positions the human body is capable of, so we've blocked the program from adjusting beyond certain angles. It's about pleasure, not torture, after all."

"Of course," Sheridan says. "Show me Sarah's limit, if you don't mind. I want to see her gorgeous snatch spread as wide as it will go—if that's all right with you, Sarah."

The fact that he's such a gentleman about it makes his question even hotter.

"I'm pretty flexible," I say, then nod to Jude, who taps the screen again.

When I met them back at their place before coming to the club, they showed me all the possible positions and let me exclude any I didn't think I'd be able to endure. I used to do gymnastics in high school, along with cheerleading, and I kept up with my training, so there weren't many I opted out of.

The rings shift again, the wires holding my harness tightening and lifting me while the ones controlling my limbs raise my arms and legs once more. This time, the machine pulls my legs out to the sides, arranging me into a full split with my arms high above my head. The difference between this and an actual split is that all my weight is supported by the cables attached to my harness. My core throbs with the exposure, and I'm almost positive I'm in danger of dripping.

Sheridan sits forward, fully engaged in the transformation taking place. He's still looking at my pussy, but lifts his gaze after a moment. "You have *the* most beautiful vulva and clitoris I have ever seen. I'm glad you don't shave it bare like most women in the scene. It is nicely trimmed and well-kept. So perfect. May I get a closer look?"

"Please do," I say. I practically hold my breath when he stands, pausing to carefully adjust his erection. He catches me watching him and smirks.

"It's a hazard of my profession. I'm used to it," he says.

"But I suspect you're quite new to this, aren't you?"

"Today's my first time really visiting the club," I say. "My best friend is a performer here, though—Casey. Did you see her show last night?"

He comes closer, nodding. "She's the one with the two Doms and the ropes. They put on quite the show, don't they? But then, so do you. This…" He pauses at the edge of the platform and waves a hand at the machine. "This is magnificent. *You* are magnificent. And the trust you have for Simon and Jude… I'm looking forward to watching the three of you."

As if on cue, the machine begins to move again, and I glance at Jude, because I didn't see him touch the screen.

"Some positions are timed," he explains. "The machine automatically returns to the default position if we don't change to a different one within a certain timeframe." He taps the screen and the machine halts again, keeping me spread wide, but with my knees bent. I'm no less exposed to them, though.

Sheridan ascends the steps onto the platform and stops next to Jude, looking over his shoulder at the tablet. "Ingenious. Can you raise her up?"

"Some," Jude says. "We're limited by the height of the machine, of course. If you're thinking what I'm thinking, the best option is either position twenty-five or sixty-nine."

Sheridan chuckles. "I can guess what sixty-nine looks like, so show me twenty-five."

He taps the screen again. The circles of the machine shift and whir, and I find myself turned face down, my arms behind my back. My hips come up and my shoulders go down, and the wires hoist my entire body higher and higher, until my face is level with Simon's where he stands, watching intently.

"You good?" he asks.

"Yeah. This is new. I didn't know it went this high."

"You are men after my own heart," Sheridan says, chuckling. I crane my head to see him and Jude, who are both eyeing me from below with devious interest. "One of you *please* go demonstrate so I can have a full picture. Your girl needs more attention, and it's clear the machine can only accommodate her to a point."

"We haven't shown you the accessories yet, but you're right," Jude says, then nods at his twin.

Simon begins by taking my face in both his hands and drawing me close for a deep and hungry kiss. His grip pulls me forward, then leaves me swinging slightly when he releases me. I giggle at the way my entire body sways on the wires.

"This is so much fun," I say. "Now who's taking care of my other end?" I peer over my shoulder at the other two still standing off to the side, my gaze lingering on Sheridan for a moment before I look at Jude, eyebrows raised.

Jude chuckles and shakes his head, then gestures toward my backside. "Be our guest, Sheridan. You should have the full experience."

Sheridan stares at Jude in what looks like shock for a moment, and I worry that we've somehow crossed a line. But he's still hard, and when he slowly turns his head to look at me, his cheeks are pink.

"Was this your idea, Sarah?" he asks in a forced tone of caution, as if he doesn't quite believe the offer.

"The twins and I like trying new things together. And this is all *very* new to me."

"If you don't want to…" Simon begins, but Sheridan raises a hand, silencing him. His gaze remains fixed on me, and he takes a few steps closer until he's standing beside

Simon, looking into my eyes. This close and from this angle, I can make out the barest of laugh lines at the corners of his eyes, and a glimmer of silver in his hair. He's probably older than the twins think, but if anything, that makes him even sexier.

"You don't know me, pet," he says in a low voice. "Are you sure you want to open that door? You're safe with your two lovers. You don't know if you'll be safe with me."

"Will you hurt me if I surrender to you?" I ask, painfully aware that I'm literally in no position to do anything *but* surrender right now.

He smirks. "Only if that's what you want me to do. But you and I aren't the only ones involved." He looks first at Simon, who's studying him intently from one side, then at Jude, who's silently watching our exchange from the other. "If I read this correctly, the three of you are a package deal. I won't get between you. But the best way to ensure I don't is for me to sample *all* the goods."

Simon's cheeks darken. His gaze flits to mine, then to the floor, and he lets out a nervous chuckle. "Are you seriously propositioning me and my brother?"

Sheridan shrugs and makes an expansive gesture. "Why shouldn't I? You're offering me a taste of the woman you clearly both love—or *she's* offering and you're allowing it. It's a dangerous game that I know better than to involve myself in. The problem is, I desperately want to take her up on her offer. If I do, I want one of *you* in the machine next, for me to play with."

My eyes widen and I stare at Simon, expecting him to adamantly refuse. Instead he just scratches his chin and smiles, then grins at Jude.

"We might have to flip a coin to see who gets the honors."

CHAPTER FIFTEEN

"The three of you are a dream come true," Sheridan says. "Truly. But just to be clear, do I have carte blanche to touch you, Sarah? Only to give you pleasure, of course."

I dart a glance at Simon, still surprised neither he nor Jude objected to being Sheridan's plaything later. If anything, he looks even more excited than he did before, with color high on his cheeks. He swallows and gives me a slight nod. "We have a new toy, baby. We may as well enjoy him."

This comment makes Sheridan laugh. "If that's the way you want to think of me, I won't object, but I do have a mind of my own. And right now, I'd very much like to kiss your girl."

"Okay," I say, a little giddy myself now.

Sheridan's eyes turn molten when he steps forward and cups my chin, holding me still as he captures my lips. His kiss is a long, slow, savoring thing, and he tastes like champagne. The swipe of his tongue sends a fresh wave of heat to my core. I lose myself for a moment, moaning when he darts his tongue past my lips for a taste.

I'm breathless when he releases me and stands back, then begins loosening his tie. He sheds it and his jacket, then kicks off his shoes and pulls off his socks. He glances at Simon, and Simon nods, picking up Sheridan's clothes once he's stripped down to his boxer briefs. Then Simon disappears toward the dressing room, leaving me staring at Sheridan, who comes close again.

He cups my cheek, caressing it with his thumb before coasting his hand down my arm as he continues to move along my side. I get the sense he's inspecting me when he pauses and cups one breast where it hangs, giving my nipple a gentle pinch before doing the same to the other breast.

My intake of breath is loud enough to make him pause, and he teases my nipples a moment longer. "Do you like this?" he asks.

"Yes. Where is Jude?"

"I'm here," Jude says. "Just enjoying the show for now. We heard you were the life of the party last night, Sheridan."

Sheridan turns to look at him. "Was I, then? I only know I rarely get the opportunity to show my true colors. This club is perfect, but we don't have anyplace quite like it in San Francisco. Many come close, but you wouldn't find a room like this in the ones I'm aware of, and I've been to almost all of them."

"Only almost?" I ask.

"There are a few that cater to women only. Naturally I'm not invited to those."

"You should open one," I suggest. "I would come. I live in the Bay area."

He tweaks my nipple once more before moving on, continuing his slow perusal of my body, sliding his hand down my back and over my hip.

"Are you sure? You're very new to the scene. You might decide it isn't for you."

"This is the second time today I've been strapped into this machine. It's safe to say I'd fit in."

"You have me there," he says. He rests a hand on one ass cheek, and my core tingles in anticipation of his attention.

Simon returns then and comes to stand at my head. He lifts an eyebrow to check in, and I start to respond, but my words disappear on a gasp when Sheridan grabs both my cheeks, spreads me open, and buries his tongue deep inside me. I give an involuntary jerk, and Simon reaches up and grabs my shoulders to steady me.

Then Sheridan withdraws his tongue, and the next thing I feel are his lips wrapped around my clit. He makes an almost primal sound in response to my whimper as he begins to tease my clit, rolling it around as if it's a piece of candy. I can't breathe, it feels so good—not just the attention to my clit, but being restrained and suspended.

I see double for a moment until I realize both twins are now standing before me. Jude leans in to kiss me while Simon begins teasing my nipples. Then I lose myself completely to their touch. The twins don't sit idle after that; while Sheridan indulges himself in my pussy, Jude keeps teasing my nipples, and Simon produces one of the bottles of oil from the dressing room, upends it over my back, and begins to rub it over every inch of exposed skin.

Sheridan releases my clit for a moment, long enough to allow me to take a breath. "Here," he says, and I have no idea what he means until I feel a warm trickle of fluid hit my exposed asshole. "That's right, let's get her loosened up everywhere. Do you like your arse played with, Sarah?"

I try to choke out a response, but my mind is mush.

Jude laughs. "She loves it. But be gentle. We already fucked her once today."

"Then she'll be extra-sensitive. We'll take care," Sheridan says. "Will you suck her clit, Simon? I want to make her come so I can see it happen up close."

"It would be my pleasure," Simon says in a low voice.

I'm lost again when Simon moves beneath my pelvis, which is at the exact height for him to reach my pussy with his mouth. He tongues my clit as Sheridan draws a spiral around and around my tight rear opening. I relax for him as he pushes a thick digit into me. It must be his thumb, as substantial as it feels. Then he twists it and inserts three fingers into my pussy.

"You are a natural at this," Sheridan says as he slowly fucks my ass and pussy with expert strokes. Jude moves forward far enough that I can rest my forehead on his shoulder, but he never lets up his teasing of my breasts.

All I can do is moan and squirm through their torment, and it only takes a moment longer before I'm flying, my body quivering in the straps as my orgasm consumes me. Sheridan keeps fingerfucking me, but slows down a little, and I can just feel him taking in every second of my climax and whatever my pussy must look like while it's happening.

They retreat slowly, Jude leaving first to retrieve the tablet while Simon gives my clit one last lick and Sheridan withdraws his fingers. The latter bends down to give my open pussy one last, long kiss as if saying farewell to a lover.

"I have a position in mind to try next and want to see if your machine can accommodate it. Sarah, do you need a breather?"

I'm in a daze as I respond with a shake of my head. "Yes, but I'm comfortable right here. It's like resting in a hammock, except my ass is hanging out."

Sheridan returns to my head and looks into my eyes. I can't help but fixate on how flushed he is now, especially his mouth. His body is taut, every muscle defined as if ready for action. I can't wrap my head around what's happening to me today; all I know is that I'm having the time of my life, and as long as the twins are game to keep going, I am.

"We'll wait a few minutes. Let us know if you need to be unfastened."

Jude taps the screen, and the machine moves, lowering me again and rotating my body into a more or less prone position with my torso slightly elevated. The wires at the back of the harness are covered in thick padding where they extend past my shoulders, providing the perfect headrest, and I let myself hang.

Sheridan moves to Jude's side to confer about whatever crazy position they plan to put me in next. I half-listen, my ears perking up when I hear one of them mutter, "…all fuck her…" which gives me another giddy rush.

Simon slips around to face me, crouching and curling his fingers around my calves, giving them a squeeze.

"You're soaking through your pajamas," I comment, too loopy from the insane orgasm I just had to filter myself.

He glances down at his crotch and chuckles at the spreading stain of pre-cum making the silk cling to the head of his cock. "I guess I got a little turned on."

"Do you even need those? You're all about to fuck me, right?"

Keeping his gaze locked on mine, he stands, hooks his thumbs in his waistband, and pushes his pants down over his hips. The elastic snags on his cock and the hard shaft comes free, smacking against his belly. The mere sight of him naked warms my core again, and I sigh in utter bliss.

"I'm so lucky I found you two again," I say. "Everything

about today is perfect, but especially getting to share this with you and Jude."

Simon rises to his knees and leans between my thighs, grabbing the handholds above me to support himself, revealing an alternate purpose to that feature. Brushing his lips over my cheek, he groans.

"This is beyond my wildest dreams, Sarah. You have no idea how perfect today has been for me too."

Then his mouth comes down on mine, and I lose my breath again as he kisses me.

The cables linked to my arms give just enough for me to slide my fingers through his hair and deepen our kiss. He rocks his hips forward, his hot shaft grazing my wet core. I wasn't sure I could get aroused again so fast, but when our skin slides against one another's, I moan and tilt my hips toward him.

"Please fuck me. I want you inside me," I whisper, which earns me another groan, and he pulls back, glancing at the other two. "Do you really need to wait for them to decide?"

He smirks. "It'll be more fun for all of us if I do. But that doesn't mean we can't enjoy ourselves while I'm here."

He leans back, then dips his head to suck one of my nipples into his mouth. At the same time, he drifts a hand between my thighs and cups my pussy. His fingers sink into me easily while he applies pressure to my clit with the heel of his palm. I'm throbbing within seconds, aching for more.

"Okay, you two," Jude says in an amused tone. "This is a group activity, so no one-on-one. Simon, back up so we can get her into position."

Simon gives me a wistful look as he stands and steps back, sighing. "Fine. Which one did you decide on?"

"One seventy-seven," Jude says, grinning and rubbing his hands together.

Simon's expression shifts instantly to a gleeful smile, and my stomach turns a flip.

"I'm not sure whether to be terrified or excited," I say.

"Excited, pet," Sheridan says, approaching as the machine begins to rearrange my limbs. "Because if we pull this off, it's going to blow *all* our minds."

CHAPTER SIXTEEN

I can't lie—it does feel like I'm on a theme park ride. I'm being carried to a magical wonderland of pleasure, my body only a toy.

The machine comes to a gentle stop, and I'm situated horizontally, my body facing the mirror on the opposite wall. It's the first time I've had this vantage and what I see is both shocking and beautiful. My face is flushed, my braid dangling toward the floor. My lower leg is bent, knee pulled up close to my chest while my other leg is lifted high, knee bent at a right angle, my ankle positioned parallel to the floor. And my pussy is spread so wide I can see the glistening wetness coating every pink fold from here.

Jude comes over and adjusts the straps near my neck so I have a soft little hammock for my head to rest on, but when he does, I realize why they chose this position. His half-hard cock is exactly at eye-level, or should I say *mouth*-level. Which means the other end of me is right where the other two need it to be. Simon and Sheridan stand to either side, and their eager gazes make my body warm in anticipation.

Jude squats to look me in the eye. "Everything good? I can release your arms, if you want."

I flex my hands and arms against the straps still binding them behind me and shake my head. "I have good circulation. I'm ready."

He nods and grins.

"Jude..." I say as he's getting up.

"What is it, baby?" He squats again, raising a hand to rest it on the crown of my head.

"Just make sure you don't block my view of the mirror. I want to see."

He smirks and glances over his shoulder. "That's what it's there for, but I see what you mean. I'll stay out of the way for now."

He moves behind me, resting a hand on my shoulder, then sliding it down to cup one breast and pinch my nipple. I watch our reflections, hyperconscious of how exposed, how immobilized I am, then watch as Simon and Sheridan close in on me.

Simon approaches my head first, bending to kiss me, then kneeling near my breasts. He lavishes them with attention, sucking and fondling until I'm flushed and panting.

My gaze drifts to Sheridan, who has grasped my foot where it's suspended overhead. He squeezes it lightly, then coasts his hand down my lower leg, over my knee, and down my thigh. It isn't until he pauses and lifts his other hand that I realize he's holding a bottle of lube. He squirts some into his palm, then hands it to Jude, who sets it aside.

He's quiet at first, until he covers two fingers in the lube and slides them between my ass cheeks. He probes carefully at my rear opening, watching my face intently. If I could spread wider, I would, because the gentle tease just makes me crave full penetration.

"Tell me what you like, pet," he says in a low voice. "Do you want me to fuck this tight little arse of yours?" He pushes the tip of one finger past the barrier and sensation explodes through me, making me gasp. Sheridan chuckles, withdrawing his fingertip, then pushing two in a second later. "I want to hear you say it, Sarah."

I'm about to blurt out the words when Simon's slow kisses make it to my pelvis. He runs his tongue across the hood of my clit, then gently grasps it between his teeth, and I lose all sense of restraint.

"God, I want you both to fuck me so bad. I want your hard cock in my ass now, please!"

Sheridan hums, twisting his fingers in my backside. He pulls them out and inserts them again with a fresh coating of lube, gives a few strokes, then wraps the hand holding the remaining lube around his cock, coating it liberally until the clear fluid drips off his balls. Then he grasps my upper ass cheek and moves in.

My pussy throbs and heats in anticipation, and my eyes flutter closed as he presses the tip of his cock to my rear entrance.

Jude strokes my head and bends down, coaching me to relax, but I'm prepared. Being completely restrained makes it easy to let go, to keep my body loose, despite an unbearable need to push back against the prodding shaft working its way into me.

Sheridan moves slowly, carefully, every gentle push and withdraw moving him deeper. I want to tell him to just shove it in, but I kind of love the way this feels too, especially with Simon's tongue gently lapping at my pussy. Slow is better, because I want all three of them filling me before I give in completely to the pleasure.

My head is buzzing from it already, Sheridan's cock gradually filling me until I finally feel his balls resting soft against my skin. I only partly make out a murmur that I realize is directed at Simon. "Your turn, mate," I think is what he says, which makes sense since Simon stands then and rests a hand against my upraised thigh.

"You ready for another dick inside you, baby?"

"Uh-huh," I whimper, resisting the urge to squirm against Sheridan, who is holding too damn still right now.

He moves into position, and all I see in the mirror is his tight ass and muscular, tattooed back, but I fixate on the scene, watching every muscle flex as he presses his cock to my slick entrance. He lets out a groan as he slides in, as quick and smooth as a hot knife through butter, and just as satisfying.

"Ohhh," I groan. "Oh god, yes. Please, please fuck me. Please don't hold back."

The two of them lock eyes, and Sheridan bites his lower lip as he slides back out, one hand gripping my foot again and the other squeezing my ass. Simon reaches down and grips my other ankle. He pulls, and the cable gives just enough for him to hook my knee over his hip to get a better angle. It's tight; he and Sheridan have very little room to maneuver.

"You can touch me," Sheridan says, pausing when Simon hesitates about where to put his other hand. Sheridan grabs Simon's wrist and places his hand on his shoulder. Simon utters a breathless "okay," then a soft groan as they both find a rhythm that's so delicious I close my eyes just to *feel* them.

When I open them again, the two are practically embracing, their gazes shifting between each other's faces and the place where their cocks are sliding in and out of me in perfect synchronicity. Jude's watching too, an inscrutable look on his face, but the pair don't seem to register our interest.

"Kiss him," I say, blurting the command to the mirror. I'm not even sure who I'm directing it to, but they both glance at me for a beat, then react in unison. They shove into me hard as they lean in, and it's the hottest thing I've seen all day. They grapple one-handed, still holding onto me with their other hands, still fucking me so well I have trouble focusing. It takes Jude's grip on my chin for me to tear my attention away.

"I'm sure you're enthralled, but it's my turn now. Open up for me, baby."

I tilt my head toward him and am faced with his glorious erection, pre-cum weeping from his tip. He holds his cock in front of me and I extend my tongue, grateful for something to focus on to help delay my inevitable crumbling from the pair of dicks bent on destroying my will.

He makes an impatient noise as I tease my tongue through his slit, and I dart a sly look at him. "You're desperate to fuck my throat, aren't you?"

"Been thinking about it all fucking day," he says. "We've never done it like this. Can you handle it?"

"I want to swallow you whole, Jude. Do it."

He grasps my braid and uses it to leverage my head toward his pelvis. I open my mouth as wide as I can, already salivating more than I thought possible. I've always adored sucking them off, and I have practiced suppressing my gag reflex to take a man deeper when I do. But in reality, every time I practiced, I thought of what I would do if I had the two of them together again.

This particular scenario never crossed my mind, but I'm ready when he pushes into my mouth so far the instinct to swallow kicks in. I close my eyes and force a breath through my nose, willing my throat to relax so he can go deeper.

"Jesus fucking Christ, Sarah," he mutters. "I didn't realize you could be even more perfect."

I have to concentrate to maintain control, the bombardment of sensations making it difficult. One of the other two has started rubbing my clit, and I moan around Jude's cock, which makes him curse and hold my braid even tighter.

"Don't want to hurt you," he murmurs. "But I need to… *fuck.*"

I give him a gentle suck, the only way I can signal that I want him to lose control, and he does. He pulls my braid to the point of pain, shoving his cock deeper until tears stream from my eyes and saliva starts to dribble from the corner of my mouth. At my other end, Sheridan and Simon are grunting as they fuck me harder, and I am so fucking close, but I can't let myself lose control with Jude so deep in my throat.

But suddenly he grunts my name, and the underside of his cock spasms against my tongue, the only warning I have that he's coming. I barely have time to prepare before his hot, sweet cum is coating the back of my throat.

He pulls out, leaving me gasping, and finishes himself with several quick, slapping strokes, aiming for my open mouth, but hitting my cheek with half of it. I'm already losing myself to the other two, though, and now that I can breathe properly, I let go.

"Oh, fuck yes! Hard, like that," I say, though Simon and Sheridan don't really need to be told. They're lost to their own momentum, and whoever's rubbing my clit rubs faster as their tempo increases. They're holding onto the backs of each other's necks, foreheads pressed together, both fixated on where their cocks are plunging into me.

"Want to see you cum first, mate," Sheridan says. "Want to watch your cream dripping off her pussy."

"Fuck, dude," Simon pants. "You fucking got it." Then he thrusts a few more times, groans, and freezes, his shaft pulsing inside me.

Sheridan pauses and breathes, "God yes, like that. I can feel your cock against mine. So bloody hot."

Simon's orgasm fades and he eases out of me. "This what you wanted to see?" he asks, crouching low. I can finally see my pussy again in the mirror as he drags his fingers through the mess he made, then stands again, raising his slick fingers to Sheridan's mouth. The other man opens and sucks them in, moaning around them as he starts pivoting his hips again. He sucks Simon's fingers clean, then nods.

"Now you. Suck her clean. Make her come."

Simon obeys, falling to his knees and leaning in, devouring my pussy so thoroughly I have zero chance of holding back any longer. I let go with an incoherent wail as he sucks my clit, aware of nothing but the delicious torment they're inflicting on me.

Sheridan's climax claims him at the same moment, and he slams in tight to ride it out, every single pulse of his cock a reflection of the spasms in my own body.

He pulls out slowly, sweat dripping off his face, and reaches for one of the clean towels situated conveniently within reach. As he cleans himself off, he gazes at our reflection in utter awe.

"Magnificent. You two have truly outdone yourselves in every way. My only regret is that *she* isn't part of the deal, but I have a proposal for you. Please unbind this goddess so we can discuss business."

CHAPTER SEVENTEEN

It turns out the enormous bathroom adjoining this room is equipped with a large shower and a hot tub. The four of us rinse off, then slip into the bubbling tub with the bottle of champagne we've barely touched. My limbs are sore, but in a good way, and the hot water and pulsing jets feel amazing.

Sheridan reaches for the champagne and pours as he talks.

"I think it's safe to say I'm one hundred percent sold on your contraption. I admit I would still love to play with it more, but purely for self-indulgence, not as a measure to decide whether it's worth investing in." He hands each of us a glass of bubbly. "I hope that after the fun we had, you're still interested in doing business too."

"Why wouldn't we be?" Jude asks.

He shifts his gaze to me. "It isn't every day that a potential business partner offers to share their girlfriend. In fact, this is a first."

The twins exchange a glance, and Simon grins. "It was her

idea. Trust me, we wouldn't have done it if she didn't suggest it first."

"See, this is why I think the three of you are going to make perfect business partners. You're openminded enough to understand the clientele I work with. Naturally we would need the designers on-site frequently to oversee things, so travel is a given, but are you also willing to travel to help promote the machine once it's in production? I wouldn't ask you to uproot your lives. I would cover all expenses, of course. This is how keen I am on having your cooperation and approval at every step. This is your baby. I want you involved."

He pauses and looks between us again. "Frankly, I simply *want* you. I regret that we don't have the time or stamina to keep playing tonight. I really wanted to take you up on your offer to put one of you in the machine and test it out with a male subject."

Jude chuckles and glances at his twin. "We regret it too, but after that... I think we need a little more time to recuperate."

"Understood," Sheridan says. "But if you accept my offer, please consider taking a trip to visit once I have the first machine built in the assembly shop I plan to set up in San Francisco. I'd like the three of you to christen it with me, because I absolutely intend to own one as well."

"Do you live in the city as well as do business there?" I ask. My head is buzzing with possibilities now, but I want all the details out in the open so Simon and Jude can put the pieces together without me saying it outright. I have no idea if they're willing to move, but I don't want it to be just about me.

"My home is in Pacific Heights. My business is mostly web-based, but my public-facing shop is in Haight-Ashbury."

"Huh," Jude says off-handedly, though his expression is thoughtful when he looks at me. "Don't you live near there, Sarah?"

"My place is in the Financial District," I say, cheeks warming more than the heated water can account for.

Simon eyes me with a half-smile, and I can tell he's catching on.

Sheridan blinks at me. "You don't live in New York?"

"I grew up here, but no. I'm finishing my degree at Stanford soon. I intern for a non-profit in the city, at the moment. I'll probably be going full-time when I graduate. I'm heading back at the end of the month."

"And your relationship has survived the distance? The three of you are so in sync I just assumed you'd been together for ages."

"It feels that way, doesn't it?" Jude says, eyes locked on me. "But no, Simon and I lost touch with Sarah when she left for college. We just reconnected a few days ago."

Sheridan's so surprised he sets down his glass and leans forward, shifting his gaze between the twins before landing on me again. "This sounds like a story I'd love to hear, but more importantly, how did you two let this creature slip through your fingers?"

"Youthful stupidity?" Simon offers with a contrite shrug.

"On all our parts," I add. "It's complicated. Maybe we'll tell the story sometime, but the important thing is that we're together now, right?"

I look to either side where the twins are sitting, hoping they hear my unspoken request. I don't want to mention it, because it's just too crazy a thing to ask when we've spent fewer than *two days* together since finding each other again, even though it feels like no time has passed.

Sheridan clears his throat. "Well, I have a very generous

offer for you that will hopefully sway your decision. And hopefully I get to benefit from it too." He smiles and shakes his head. "Will you stop making eyes at each other for just a minute so I can give you the actual number I have in mind?"

When we give him an expectant look, he laughs and holds up a finger. "I just need to go grab the paperwork." Then he climbs out of the tub, reaching for a towel that he slings around his waist before disappearing into the other room.

He returns a moment later with a messenger bag he must have been carrying when he arrived, but that I entirely missed in the moment. He pulls out a spiral-bound sheaf with a fancy letterhead on the first sheet and sets it at the edge of the tub beside us. I take a peek and see the name of the twins' business, along with Sheridan's in the first paragraph. He takes a moment to explain the terms to us and turns the page, pointing at the value of the partnership.

Simon barks a laugh, shaking his head in disbelief. I stare in utter shock at all the zeroes, looking for a misplaced decimal, but not finding it.

"Seriously?" Jude asks. "Why this much?"

"It's the software, frankly. I consulted with my attorneys, and they pointed out that the program you've written is unique enough to be patented. It could have other applications besides the sex industry... more lucrative ones by far, including potential medical uses. Frankly, it's worth more, but this is all I can afford, which is why I added this clause, making it clear I'd only receive a token percentage in the case of third parties licensing it for other uses. My team will assist in getting the entire thing patented with you two as dual rights holders. My part is only as agent. You have nothing to worry about."

The twins share an excited look, and my own heart is in my throat with joy for the two of them. They seem too stunned to speak, so I say, "I think they need some time to have it looked over, if that's okay."

Sheridan nods. "Absolutely. Please take your time. I'll leave this with you here." He sets the contract on the counter where it'll stay dry, then looks at us again with an affectionate smile. "I think this is my cue to give you three lovely people some space. My flight home is open-ended, so I'm here if you have any concerns."

The formality in his tone is somehow endearing, and I'm tempted to ask him to stay, because I sense he'd really like to, but doesn't want to intrude. But I need time with the twins alone.

"Thank you," Simon and Jude both say in unison, yet again signaling they're of the same mind on this. Jude adds, "We'll talk it over and call you tomorrow with our decision."

"Very well. Enjoy your evening." He starts to leave, then stops in the doorway and turns. "Ah, if I may be so bold, even if we *don't* do business together, please keep my number. I'd love to remain friends."

"That would be nice," I say, smiling at him. He nods and smiles back, then slips out the door, closing it behind him.

"Fuuuck," Jude says, sinking deeper into the water and resting his head back on the ledge.

Simon moves to the other side to face us, sitting up on the edge of the tub and leaning his elbows on his knees.

"First off, Sarah, you're the deciding factor here."

"What? I shouldn't be. Guys, you *have* to say yes!"

"He means about us moving the whole business to California, versus staying here and just traveling."

I'm dumbfounded that they're even asking, and when I stare at them without speaking for several seconds, Simon says, "Please say something."

"How... Why...?" I shake my head and take a breath, but

find it hard to speak, because this all feels too good to be true. "You already know I can't move back to New York yet, but now there's literally *no* reason that you guys shouldn't move to San Francisco. And I really hope you're not hesitating because you think I don't want you there. Of *course* I fucking want you there!"

"Well, when you put it that way..." Jude says with a sardonic smirk.

"I guess we're moving to San Francisco," Simon adds.

I shriek with joy and leap at Simon, kissing him hard. "Oh my god, this is so wonderful!" He's laughing when I turn to Jude and climb into his lap, peppering his entire face with kisses. "I love you both so much. I never even dreamed this could happen. We have to talk about it! Make plans! Oh shit, you should come with me when I go! This is perfect!"

They're both laughing now, and Simon returns to this side of the tub and sits beside his twin, grabbing my legs and pulling them across his lap.

"I kind of just want to bask in the happiness for a little while longer. Especially since your excitement is kind of a huge turn-on." Simon slides a hand up my thigh, and I open my legs a little to give him access, but wince when he gets to my tender core. His brow furrows. "Did we hurt you?"

"No, the last two days have just worn me out a little. It still feels good. I'm just sore." He nods and shifts his fingers up a little, finding my clit and lightly stroking it. Pleasure and heat pool deep inside me. "That part doesn't hurt," I say with a smile.

Jude curls an arm around my waist, raising his hand to cup one breast. "Your nipples are okay, right?" he asks, stroking a wet thumb across one.

I sigh and spread my legs wider, leaning my head on Jude's shoulder. "You guys could do this to me all night."

"I'd like that," Simon says. "But we should get out of here and take you home first. Let's press pause for now."

I let Jude lift me in his arms and carry me out of the tub.

Less than an hour later, the three of us are back at their apartment over the shop, freshly showered and tangled up in the nest they made on their floor. They make love to me carefully, but with complete focus on my pleasure. I want them both so much that it's easy to dismiss the tenderness between my legs long enough to give back to each of them the way that makes the most sense right now.

Jude is at my back when he enters me from behind, sliding in and thrusting with slow, gentle strokes. "I'm not going to last," he murmurs into my ear. "You feel so damn good."

I urge him on, and he climaxes within minutes, then Simon pushes me onto my back and slides inside. Jude remains close, taking turns kissing me with his twin until Simon's climax cascades through him like the dawn breaking, the love in his eyes every bit as brilliant as his brother's.

I drift off moments later, more satisfied and complete than I've ever felt in my life.

CHAPTER EIGHTEEN

The rest of my trip is half-crazy, half-wonderful. The twins sign the contract, and we invite Sheridan over to celebrate with Casey, Max, and Rick. We give him a tour of the shop where the machine was conceived, and I talk Simon into being our toy for an evening, much to Sheridan's delight.

The others are here for the party and too entertained to notice. Sheridan has a flair for the dramatic and makes it out to be some kind of magic show, which embarrasses Simon, and I get the sense this is his first time with a true audience. But Casey and her Doms are like family, so he gets into it quickly.

"Do you want to go next?" I ask Jude when I catch how aroused he is seeing his twin get nailed by our new friend. It's Simon's first time with a *real* dick, he explained, but he also assured Sheridan he'd "practiced" plenty, so not to go easy.

Jude gives me an amused look. "You're weirdly chill about finding out we like fooling around with men too."

I shrug. "It's just another thing to try, I guess. If you don't like it, you don't have to do it again."

He clears his throat. "Do you have an issue if we keep seeing Sheridan?"

"Not as long as you share." I nudge him with my elbow, and he slings his arm around my waist and hauls me in tight to his side.

He nuzzles my temple. "What's mine is yours, Sarah. I love you."

I relax against him with a happy sigh. Simon's in the throes of one epic orgasm when I glance back up, and Sheridan looks just as enraptured. He has Simon strapped in spread-eagle, like he's Da Vinci's Vitruvian Man, except the extra limbs belong to another man currently fucking him silly.

It's a beautiful sight, one I'm a little surprised I'm into. It never occurred to me that I'd like *watching* either of my twins being pleasured by someone else, though it might be different if it were another woman. But maybe not, because who knows? We have a whole world of kinky adventures to explore, and I am not likely to say no to anything, as long as I get to be with them and we're all having fun.

We send Sheridan home that night with the signed contract, and a promise to call him when we get to San Francisco at the end of the month. He kisses us each soundly before heading out the door when his driver arrives, looking like it pains him to have to leave.

After that night, we make *all* the plans, making love in between the twins' ongoing business calls and my afternoons rediscovering my friendship with Casey. I've never been happier.

The following weekend, we finally have dinner with my parents and sisters. My family welcomes the twins back with open arms, as if they never left. Dad takes the pair aside after dinner and apologizes for what happened, explaining things the way he explained them to me. Their foster license meant everything to them at the time, and he's sorry he didn't have a chance to cool down and explain things when it happened. But everything is different now, and my parents have always been open-minded, progressive people, which I spent too long being hurt to realize. So much pain could have been avoided with a simple conversation. Yet somehow I can't bring myself to regret the way things went anymore. Something tells me things would be very different now if I hadn't walked out of the twins' lives when I did.

All in all, it feels like everything that was broken is fixed by the time we're packing their belongings into a trailer attached to the back of my car, getting ready to make the haul back to California.

Naturally we can't haul *all* their things. Their shop equipment is too valuable not to trust to professionals, but Sheridan's contract came with an enormous influx of funds, including a generous budget for relocation. Jude and Simon try to convince me to let them buy me a new car, which prompts a lengthy conversation about boundaries and financial responsibility. Instead they spring for a bumper-to-bumper tune-up and get it detailed for me.

We've already said goodbye to the Whitewood crowd, who threw us *another* huge party complete with a show featuring the machine. One of the twins' tasks before leaving is to train several operators on how to use it so the club will always have someone on staff to maintain it. It was amazing watching different people volunteer to take the ride, then come down after having the time of their life. Jude and Simon were on hand, handing out business cards for people to get on their waiting list to own their own. I think they landed at least a dozen potential buyers that night alone.

"Look at us, literally driving into the sunset," Jude says the last evening just after another supper with my folks. The dusky road stretches before us, along with a night of driving. Since there are three of us, we've opted to drive straight through, taking shifts at the wheel, and want to start while there's less traffic to contend with.

Sheridan's at the other end, already waiting with keys to a new apartment in his neighborhood. I'm still recovering from the sticker shock after seeing the rent, but Jude and Simon are being paid enough to cover it and then some. I'm afraid to think about the money, because it's just so mind-boggling how lucky they are, how filthy rich they're about to be if the business takes off the way it looks like it will. They had the contract looked over by the attorney Whitewood keeps on retainer, and she couldn't find a thing wrong with it, even going so far as to commend Sheridan for the foresight of urging them to patent their program.

I will say one thing—the two-day trip lets me become acquainted with the twins in a whole new way, and I'm happy to report that I probably love them even more. For example, Jude's a speed demon and is the biggest reason we made such good time, but he only speeds when Simon's napping, because his twin is the biggest stickler for traffic laws, something I never knew about either of them.

I already knew they had beautiful singing voices, but didn't know they both know all the words to the songs on the latest Taylor Swift album. And they discovered that I'm an absolute wiz at trivia games, and kicked their asses all the way from Chicago to Cheyenne. They're the *worst* sore losers too, but after a couple back-seat BJs, I earned their forgiveness.

I'm still pinching myself when we finally arrive in San Francisco after the grueling trip. It's the middle of the night, but Sheridan's already on the street, waving us down and directing us into his own driveway, which is a blessing since he lives on a hill and I have no idea how to park a trailer on this steep a slope.

"You made it!" he says, beaming at is as we extract ourselves from the car and stare around to get our bearings.

"We sure did. My god, is this where you live?" I ask, staring up at the enormous Victorian house that looms above us. It probably has a view of the entire city from its upper floors.

"Welcome to my humble home. Come in, I have a room for you—or *rooms,* if that's what you'd prefer. I won't assume to know how you like to sleep, but I hope to learn."

"Right now, I just want to be horizontal for about a week," Jude says, looking just as worn out as I feel.

Sheridan leads us up a set of steps to his front door and inside a beautiful, yet understated foyer. Despite the fancy architecture, the interior fits him well, though it's evident he's rich from the quality and refinement of the décor. He doesn't flaunt his wealth, at least, which is refreshing.

But he doesn't stop or offer a tour; he keeps going up another flight of steps off the foyer and points out an enormous bedroom with a king-sized bed.

"This is the room I set up for you. You're welcome to it, or any of the others…"

He doesn't even finish the thought before all three of us kick off our shoes. I'm first to the bed, flinging myself onto it face-down and letting out an exhausted groan.

"Oh, wow. I'm afraid if I sleep here, I'll never want to get up."

"I don't think Sher would be bothered if we decided to

live in this bedroom," Jude says, glancing toward the door. I follow his look to find Sheridan gazing back at us like his supper just arrived and he's being made to wait to eat.

"I haven't bathed in two days…" I say.

Sheridan strides across the room and opens a pair of double doors to reveal a bathroom built for a king. I'm curious enough to drag myself off the bed to go check it out. The shower is enormous, and a small Jacuzzi tub is situated in corner beneath a skylight. I pull off my shirt without even thinking, because I am *so* down with a shower right now.

"I know you'll want to move into your own place soon, but your belongings don't arrive for another week, and you'll need to buy more to fully furnish the place. I want you to be comfortable. My home is your home as long for as you need it."

I glance up at him and shake my head. "I'm in awe of you right now, you know?"

"Same here," Simon says, slipping past me and turning on the shower. The brat is already naked and climbs in with a grin.

"Hey! No fair," I say, hurriedly disrobing the rest of the way and joining him. I find a second shower head that I turn on and give Simon the finger from across the space. Sheridan laughs and leans in, reaching for another knob I missed. Above us, the ceiling starts to *rain*, hot water cascading down over the entire interior.

"Fuck yeah," Jude says, stepping in and tilting his face up, mouth open.

"I will leave you to it," Sheridan says. "Are you hungry? I'm happy to feed you before you sleep."

"Oh no you don't," I say, stepping toward him and grabbing the waistband of his jeans. "You're joining us, mister."

He looks abashed and glances at the twins, uncertain.

"Get your ass in here so we can give you a proper hello," Simon says, reaching for a bottle of body wash and soaping up his hands.

Sheridan's goosebumps are the most visible sign of his excitement as he strips, and he's already hard when he steps beneath the water. I close in and reach for him first, slipping my arms around his neck and gazing up into his eyes.

"Hello, you," I say, smiling.

He rests his hands at my hips and stares at me in utter bafflement. "Are you real? None of this feels real right now. I have spent the last few weeks wondering if I dreamed the whole encounter in New York, but I have a contract signed by the twins that says it happened. And now you're here."

"We're really here," I say, leaning up to kiss him beneath the water. He tastes like tea and gingersnaps, which is comforting, and my heart skips a beat, because somehow it adds to the sense of *coming home*, even though everything about this experience is brand new.

He hums against my mouth, then groans when I tilt my hips against his erection. When I crack my eyelids, I realize Jude's in the process of soaping up Sheridan's back. Then Simon's behind me doing the same. The twins bracket us, keeping us pressed together.

"You three are going to break me," Sheridan says. "In fact, I think you already have."

"It's okay, we'll put you back together," I say. "Because we sort of decided we want to keep you, if that's okay."

"Good god, it's more than okay. I am more than ready to be kept. But if you'll indulge me, I want the three of you washed so we can relax while we enjoy each other. Chop, chop."

He turns and grabs the body wash, then proceeds to take care of my front side, working his lathered hands from my shoulders down to my feet. He kneels and methodically massages the soap in between my toes. Jude stands behind him, soaping himself, content to watch his twin and Sheridan attend to me. Sheridan slides a soapy hand up my inner thigh and pauses, gazing up at me with a devious smile.

"I missed your beautiful snatch, Sarah. May I wash it for you?" He grazes his fingertips lightly along my outer lips just as Simon slips his hands around to cup my breasts and tease my nipples. My core warms, pulsing lightly with the promise of the attention I'm about to get.

"Lean into me, baby. Give him what he wants," Simon says.

I obey, letting myself relax against the solid strength behind me. I let Sheridan lift my left foot to his shoulder, then very gently stroke his soapy fingers between my folds. He's thorough and business-like about it, but it feels too good to be completely innocent. Then he turns his head toward Jude and tilts his chin to the wall behind him.

"Hand me the sprayer."

Jude lifts the hand-held sprayer from its holder and Sheridan takes it, rotating the dial on the nozzle until it produces the right combination of fat, pulsing streams. I clench a little in anticipation of being rinsed, but he takes his time, starting again at my shoulders and working his way down. Except this time, he pauses to focus the stream for several seconds on each nipple, and avoids my pussy entirely until after he's rinsed my feet. My core is tight and hot with need, and when he directs the stream at my pelvis, I'm already aching for it.

Jude moves close and kneels beside him, reaching out and parting my folds with two fingers. My clit is huge and swollen, and makes an easy target when Sheridan aims the spray right at it. I gasp and reach up and back, clinging to Simon's neck.

"Too much? Not enough?" Sheridan asks, twisting the spray back and forth incrementally so it's like a watery finger rubbing against my clit.

"Oh god, that's just right."

Simon nuzzles my neck. "This is so hot. I kind of don't want to sleep at all now."

"Me neither," Jude says, dipping his head to wrap his lips around one nipple. Simon cups my other breast and teases. I stare down at Sheridan, surprised by the utter adoration he has for all three of us. It's more than endearing tonight, though. My heartbeat thunders in my ears to the tempo of the pulsing water as my climax rockets through me. I could love him as much as the twins, if he's like this all the time.

I gasp a harsh cry, then reach for Sheridan. "Fuck me. Fuck me *now*."

He doesn't even hesitate, tossing the sprayer aside, heedless of the direction it points. He grabs me behind the thighs and Simon helps, lifting me up so Sheridan can slot himself against my entrance. I wrap my legs around him and moan as he slides in deep and slow.

One of the twins squeezes his hand between us and finds my clit again after a moment, so in tune with my rhythm. they know when I can come again. And I do, with Sheridan inside me, his mouth at my breast. When his climax hits, he reaches for Simon and I angle to the side to let them kiss, only to find Jude right there, taking my mouth with desperate need.

Sheridan's tempo slows and he heaves a shaky sigh, resting his forehead against mine. "I am completely and utterly shattered over you three," he says, giving me another lazy thrust.

"I'm pretty sure it's mutual," I say, tilting my chin closer to graze my lips against his.

"As mutual as it can get," Jude says. "Though we probably need to talk about ground rules, if we're going to do this right."

Sheridan draws our kiss out a little longer, moaning regretfully against my mouth before pulling away. "I agree. I wish there were three of me, but there's only one, so you lot will have to fight amongst yourselves to decide who gets me when."

He smirks at us as he steps back to rinse off. I gawk at him. Simon and Jude laugh.

But it only highlights how easy things are between us, as if the four of us were iron filings drawn to the same magnet.

I don't know who to credit, but if I had to make a wild guess, it isn't a person; it was Whitewood that brought us all together—a perfect butterfly effect that might never have occurred if not for my best friend missing her curfew one night years ago. That summer shattered the girls we'd been, the friendship we'd had. It shattered the love I'd begun to build with the twins. But while our paths took a while to converge again, they were always destined to wind up at the same place, and for us to be reforged into something even stronger.

"This is the perfect way to kick off our new life here," Simon says as we exit the bathroom wrapped in nothing but enormous fluffy towels. Jude and Sheridan are ahead of us, Jude awkwardly trying to ask Sheridan if he'll fulfill one of his fantasies tonight.

"I have a feeling this is going to *be* our life here going forward. I feel like we're the luckiest people in the world." I take Simon's hand and raise it to my lips. He pulls me against his side, and we pause at the end of the enormous bed, because the scene in front of us is too delicious to interfere with.

"Sneaky bastard," Simon says. "Sheridan promised I'd get payback for letting him fuck me. Now Jude gets to fuck him first?"

"Don't fret, love. You can all have a turn, if you like," Sheridan says over his shoulder. His ass is in the air, and Jude's drizzling clear lube right onto his puckered hole.

Sheridan winks and lifts one hand, a giant strap-on dildo dangling from it.

I laugh and leap on the bed. "You, sir, are the *best* sex toy a girl could ask for. I am most definitely going to keep you."

ABOUT OPHELIA BELL

Ophelia Bell loves a good bad-boy and especially strong women in her stories. Women who aren't apologetic about enjoying sex and bad boys who don't mind being with a woman who's in charge, at least on the surface, because pretty much anything goes in the bedroom.

Ophelia grew up on a rural farm in North Carolina and now lives in Los Angeles with her own tattooed bad-boy husband and six attention-whoring cats.

Subscribe to Ophelia's newsletter to get updates directly in your inbox. If newsletters aren't your thing, you can find her on social media.

http://opheliabell.com/subscribe

facebook.com/AuthorOpheliaBell
twitter.com/OpheliaDragons

ALSO BY OPHELIA BELL

Sleeping Dragons Series

Animus

Tabula Rasa

Gemini

Shadows

Nexus

Ascend

Sleeping Dragons Omnibus

Rising Dragons Series

Night Fire

Breath of Destiny

Breath of Memory

Breath of Innocence

Breath of Desire

Breath of Love

Breath of Flame and Shadow

Breath of Fate

Sisters of Flame

Rising Dragons Omnibus

Dragon's Melody (a standalone dragon novel)

Immortal Dragons Series

Dragon Betrayed

Dragon Blues

Dragon Void

Dragon Splendor

Dragon Rebel

Dragon Guardian

Dragon Blessed

Dragon Equinox

Dragon Avenged

Immortal Dragons Box Sets:

Immortal Dragons: Books 1, 2, & 3 + Prequel

Immortal Dragons: Books 4-6 + Epilogue

Black Mountain Bears

Clawed

Bitten

Nailed

Stonetree Trilogy

Fate's Fools Series

Deva's Song (Fate's Fools Prequel)

Fate's Fools

Fool's Folly

Fool's Paradise

Fool's Errand

Nobody's Fool

Eye of the Hurricane

Fool's Bargain

April's Fools

Thieves of Fate

Aurora Champions Series

(Set in Milly Taiden's "Paranormal Dating Agency" world)

The Way to a Bear's Heart

Hot Wings

Triple Talons

Midnight Star

Once in a Dragon Moon

Rebel Lust Erotica

Casey's Secrets

Blackmailing Benjamin

Burying His Desires

Doubling Down

Second Skin Series

Mad Dog

Mile High

Valentine's Day

The Devil's Daughter

Marked Man

Standalone Erotic Tales

After You

Out of the Cold